BOOKER & FITCH MYSTERIES: BOOK 3

MURDER at Midnight

LIZ HEDGECOCK PAULA HARMON

WHITE RHINO BOOKS

ISBN-13: 979-8853460928

To our parents,
who encouraged a love of reading

CHAPTER 1

Jade Fitch strolled down the high street of Hazeby-on-Wyvern carrying a hot chocolate, a milky coffee, and a paper bag with two Danish pastries. Though she wore one of her favourite outfits, a black tiered skirt with twinkling mirrors and a purple velvet ruched top, and despite the blue sky and pavements sparkling with remnants of early frost as if they had secrets to tell, she felt rather flat. Not even volunteering for the elevenses snack run had lifted her mood. She pushed open the door of Crystal Dreams with her elbow and went in.

Netta was talking to a customer. Not their usual clientele, but a man in a navy suit whose back view looked middle-aged. 'We've got some lovely silver pendants,' she was saying.

Jade put Netta's hot chocolate and the paper bag on the end of the counter. 'Anything I can help with?'

‘Our customer is looking for a Christmas present for his wife,’ said Netta. ‘Apparently she’s a fan of the shop.’

‘It’s her favourite,’ said the customer. ‘She visits whenever she’s in Hazeby and she’ll love a gift from here. The problem is that she’s already got most of the things you sell.’

A fan of the shop! Jade had never dreamt that one day she might own an establishment which had fans. But that didn’t solve the present problem. ‘What sort of budget do you have?’ she asked. ‘What does she usually buy from the shop?’

‘Up to a hundred pounds, and I’m not sure. She has a cauldron and a spell book, and I’ve definitely seen her wear a silver necklace with a four-leaf clover on it.’

Along with half the population of Hazeby, thought Jade, remembering the good-luck charm craze sparked by certain events in October. ‘How about crystals?’ she said, eyeing one of the amethyst geodes in the window. ‘They’re good for all sorts of things. They can enhance creativity, or health, or romance…’

The man swallowed. ‘Perhaps creativity? She’s always talking about writing a novel or painting watercolours, or doing linocuts, whatever those are.’

‘In that case, I would definitely recommend amethyst,’ said Jade, walking to the window and picking up one of the geodes. ‘I’d normally price this at a hundred and fifty, but as it's Christmas I'm prepared to do you a special deal. One hundred pounds and it's yours.'

'Umm…'

'And I'll write you a card to go with it, explaining its powers.'

'Oh yes, she'll like that.' The man felt inside his jacket and brought out his wallet. 'I don't suppose you'd gift wrap it, would you?'

'Of course. Once you've paid, you can choose a card from our display.' She glanced at Netta, whose eyebrows were halfway up her forehead.

'Great.' He touched his card to the reader, then trotted after Jade to the card rack, where he chose a card featuring a sassy-looking black cat wearing a purple bow tie and drop earrings.

Once he had gone, cradling his purchase, Jade puffed out a satisfied sigh. 'I never thought I'd see the day when one of those geodes finally left the shop.'

'I can't believe you gave him such a big discount,' said Netta. 'Before Christmas, too!'

'I wouldn't usually,' said Jade. 'But a hundred is more than I paid for it, and I'd prefer the money in the bank.'

'We're still selling quite a lot,' said Netta.

'True, but not as much as we did around Halloween and Bonfire Night. Then again, I suppose that's our Christmas. The thing is, I've been ordering stock in for New Year. Lots of crystals and self-help books. Motivational stuff, to tempt people who've made a load of New Year's resolutions.'

'That doesn't sound very witchy,' said Netta, and pouted.

'It isn't,' said Jade. 'But we're not just a witchy shop. If there's money to be made by flogging books called *Heal Your Life* or *Your 30-Day Life Coach*, I have every intention of making it.' Her brow furrowed for a moment. 'I should probably tell Fi what I'm doing. Give her a chance to get New Year stuff in, if she hasn't already thought of it.' She sighed. 'I wish I could come up with a new product for people to buy in the run-up to Christmas. Something nowhere else has.'

'Good luck with that,' said Netta, taking the top off her hot chocolate and sipping carefully.

'I know. I've probably left it too late.' Jade drank some coffee and fished a Danish pastry out of the bag. 'Having Hugo to stay over Christmas is messing with my head. Instead of thinking about stock or special offers, I keep wondering whether he's turned vegan and forgotten to mention it, or whether I should take the sofa and let him have my bed, or whether he'll like his present.' She bit into the pastry and chewed meditatively.

'I'm sure it'll be fine,' said Netta. 'I mean, he's your son. I can't wait to meet him. How old did you say he was again?'

'Twenty-four. Or possibly twenty-five: I lose track. We don't see each other often, so I want to make it special.' She paused, debating whether to say what was on her mind, and decided to lance the boil. 'I'm worried that now he has loads of university friends who are clever and quirky and funny and probably loaded, I'll seem a bit dull.'

Netta smiled. 'You could never be dull.'

'Huh. I'm pretty sure I thought my mum was dull when I was in my twenties, so it's just the cycle of life.'

'The cycle of life...' said Netta, gazing into the distance. 'That's so deep.'

'Or history repeating itself, if you prefer. Now, what I would like to repeat is selling the other flaming geode. When you've finished your brew, Netta, would you mind taking a look at the window display? We could pop the other geode in the middle and slap an offer label on it. And if you do manage to flog it, I'll pay you a Christmas bonus.'

Netta's eyes widened. 'Really?'

'Yep. Sell that geode for a hundred pounds or more and I'll add a tenner to your pay packet.' Jade figured an incentive wouldn't hurt – and besides, Netta didn't know that she was getting a Christmas bonus anyway.

'Right,' said Netta. She drained her hot chocolate and slammed the paper cup down on the counter.

'You're on.'

'What about your Danish pastry?' said Jade. 'You can't leave it here, alone and defenceless, because I *will* eat it.' She took a big bite of her own pastry to demonstrate.

'I'll put it in the fridge.' Netta picked up the bag and went into the back room. She was gone for a couple of minutes, and when she returned she had a gleam in her eye. 'You definitely can't pinch it now. I've put a spell on it.'

Jade laughed. 'Have you?'

'Yes,' said Netta proudly. 'Anyone who eats that pastry will get a stomachache.'

Jade thought this over. 'Well, if I eat two Danish pastries in a row, I probably will get a stomachache. Out of interest, can you lift the spell?'

Netta's mouth dropped open. 'No,' she said, in hushed tones. 'I haven't got to that page yet.'

'Never mind,' said Jade. 'I can probably fix it for you when you've finished dealing with the window. I'm just popping upstairs for a few minutes, if that's OK.'

'Sure,' said Netta. 'I'll go outside, take a picture of the window with my phone, and work out what to do.'

'Good idea.'

Jade climbed the stairs to her flat, suppressing her giggles over Netta's cursed Danish pastry. *As long as it doesn't spread to my ham and cheese sandwich*, she thought, and allowed herself a proper laugh at the idea of unwrapping her lunch to find it glaring at her.

She stopped laughing as she let herself into the flat. It wasn't awful: heaven knows, she and Hugo had lived in much worse places, with rising damp, leaking ceilings, and nonexistent hot water. But it wasn't homely. Now that the shop was making good money on a consistent basis, Jade had allowed herself a few luxuries – a rug in the sitting room, thicker curtains – but the walls were still landlord magnolia and the furniture flatpack. It looked more like a student house than the home of a responsible adult. *If that's what I am. I suppose it had to happen sometime.*

She sighed as she surveyed her home. *At least it's clean.* She plumped a sagging cushion. *It's only for a few days. Hugo will have to lump it.*

Maybe you should make a new year's resolution to get this place how you want it.

Yeah, right, thought Jade. *That won't happen unless I can think of a great money-spinning idea to take advantage of last-minute Christmas shoppers.* She gazed around her again and her heart sank. The walls seemed to be closing in. *I have to get out of here.*

She clattered downstairs, glad that her next-door neighbour Rick would be in his shop and hopefully unable to hear her, and went back to Crystal Dreams. Netta was sitting at the counter, staring at her phone and frowning. 'Just nipping out for a bit,' said Jade.

Netta transferred the frown to her. 'You were out only a few minutes ago.'

'I need inspiration,' said Jade. 'And I should tell Fi about my new-year plans for the shop. Besides, that will give you a clear run on selling the geode. I wouldn't want to cramp your style.'

'True,' said Netta, looking at her suspiciously. 'When you get back, we're running low on black-cat wrapping paper. Still got plenty of witches on broomsticks, but everyone wants the cats.'

'I'll put it on order for next-day delivery,' said Jade, shrugging on her swishy black coat and jamming a purple fedora on her dark curls. 'See you in a bit.' And without waiting for a goodbye, she left the shop and strode down the road towards the Book Barge.

CHAPTER 2

On the Book Barge, Fi re-entered figures on a spreadsheet for the third time. She'd begun to lose track of what she was trying to work out.

Oblivious to this, her assistant Nerys was in full flow as she tidied the Christmas display. 'So I turn around and say, "It is what it is, hon. As the famous wise Frenchman said, *que sera sera*." And *she* turns around and says— Oh hello, Mrs Brummell! How are you? Would you like a hand down the steps?'

'No thank you, Nerys.' The older woman descended into the shop at a speed that made Fi twitch and wonder where the first-aid kit was. 'I'm probably more nimble than you. The last time you came to keep fit, I thought you and your friend were going to keel over after five minutes. My friend and I were barely out of breath.'

'That was three years ago,' retorted Nerys. 'I'd not

long had a baby. We do dancercise now.'

'No stamina, you girls,' said Mrs Brummell. 'If you'd had to manhandle the pram I had for my little Mark in 1974, your stomach would have been back to normal in no time.'

Nerys stood up straight and breathed in, a slight scowl on her normally amiable face.

If Mrs Brummell noticed, she didn't comment. 'Good morning, Fi.' She peered over the counter at the columns of figures. 'Doing sums? You'd be better off with a piece of paper.'

'Quite possibly,' said Fi. Her phone vibrated. 'Would you mind if I took this through to the living quarters and left you with Nerys?'

'Not at all,' said Mrs Brummell. 'Now then, Nerys, talking of getting out of breath – has that Christmas special arrived yet?' She waggled her eyebrows.

'Yes,' said Nerys. 'Your copy's here.' She bent to fetch the latest steamy novel by Mrs Brummell's favourite romance author from among the reserved orders kept under the counter. 'I worry about her heart, I really do,' she murmured to Fi. 'It's not right for a woman in her seventies, reading this sort of thing. It even makes me blush.'

'"Little" Mark must have got here somehow,' whispered Fi, as she picked up her laptop and notebook.

'Don't!' Nerys went red. 'I don't want to think

about that. "Little" Mark Brummell's six foot three and his daughter's my bestie. He's too old himself for that sort of thing. Eww.' She shuddered.

Chuckling, Fi went into *Coralie*'s private quarters, put the laptop down and checked her phone. She had a message from Inspector Falconer. She still hadn't got round to changing his name in her contacts to simply Marcus. But at the end of the day, as Nerys would have said, he *was* a police inspector.

He had sent a photograph of a glass of bright liquid with a sunny beach behind it. *Safely arrived Santa Cruz last night. This beats a coffee by the Wyvern. Though grumpy teenager isn't as good company as some might be. Mostly because he hasn't surfaced yet.*

I hope that's just orange juice, Fi messaged back. *The sun's not past the yardarm in Tenerife yet. Not that I know what a yardarm is.*

Call yourself a seafarer? he replied. *And I refuse to answer re the drink. Hang on, Leo's surfaced and he's demanding breakfast. Are teenage sons ever full?*

Fi laughed as she typed. *Not that I've noticed. Have a good holiday. I'm working out the cost of keeping the Christmas lights switched on at BB.*

Ouch. Speak soon. Take care.

You too.

Fi smiled. She'd send him a picture of a cup of coffee with the sluggish Wyvern and the frosty riverside in the background later. There might not be blazing sun, a sandy beach or palm trees, but she'd bet that deep down, Marcus would be glad to come home after his holiday. And maybe that wouldn't just be because he loved his job, the lush green scenery or the ancient history, but because of something or rather someone else.

Stan the dog jumped in her lap, as he always did whenever she was about to stare at a laptop in mild despair. 'It's as well the lights on the deck are solar-powered,' she said, typing the projections into the column and checking the formulas were right. 'But it wouldn't be Christmas without lights, would it? It's not that big a dent.'

'Rrrerrfff,' woofed Stan.

Fi closed the laptop, returned to the shop and waved goodbye to Mrs Brummell as she ascended the stairs.

Nerys reached down to scratch Stan's ears. 'Are you sure you don't want me to help once school's out?'

'No, you enjoy your holiday,' said Fi. 'Children are only little once. Dylan and I will manage just fine. It'll be quiet between Christmas and New Year anyway. Um, did you really give Mrs B a paper carrier bag four times the size of the book?'

'She shouldn't be seen with that book in public,' said Nerys, pursing her lips. 'It's not right.'

'Hers was the hippy generation,' Fi reminded her. 'She probably got up to stuff that would make your hair curl. It's hard to tell when someone's always in a sensible cardigan and brogues.'

'And knows fourteen recipes for apple pie.' Nerys giggled and went to help a man who was beckoning from the Crime section.

Jade appeared at the top of the steps. 'Did someone say pie?'

'Just recipes, I'm afraid,' said Fi as her friend descended in a swirl of skirts, the coloured lights strung about the shop reflecting in the tiny mirrors sewn into the fabric. 'You're sparkly today.'

'I sold a geode.'

'Wow,' said Fi, 'I thought they'd never— I mean, well done.'

'Mmm. I wanted to discuss what we're doing for Christmas and New Year.'

'We have. Dylan and I are going to Annie's for Christmas Day, and Mum and Dad will be there too. You and Hugo can come if you like.'

Jade blinked. 'I know, but no thanks. Anyway, what I meant—'

'I thought we'd already decided to go to the party at the Duck and Druid on New Year's Eve.'

'Yes, we did. I meant from a business point of view.' Jade peered at the display of Christmas books and selected one on local midwinter legends. 'We cross over sometimes…'

'Yes, but only a bit. I have the boring stuff and you have the exciting stuff.'

'You mean serious and ridiculous.' Jade winked.

'I don't. Not all of it, anyway.'

'And yes, we always send people on to each other if they want a product outside our remit. I was thinking of something special.'

'That's all I've got and all I'll have,' said Fi, indicating her display. 'It's going well so far. Christmas releases, classics, a bit of folklore, children's books about Christmas and Hanukkah. I'll change it over from Boxing Day – New Year, New You. Diets, exercise books, hobby kits, that sort of thing. Obviously, if anyone wants detox potions or mindfulness stuff, I'll send them to you. I suppose we could have planned ahead better, but when I was ordering stuff in early November, things around here were a bit—'

'Yeah, me too. Don't worry. Next year, maybe.' Jade took a last glance at the folklore book and put it back.

Fi watched her friend wander round the shop, wondering what she was after. They already had an agreement as to how much of their stock strayed onto common ground, and kept to it, but that was just practical. On the whole, people visited the Book Barge for books and Crystal Dreams for gifts and curios.

'I'm on the hunt,' said Jade.

'I can see that. What for? A present for Hugo?' Fi had no idea what Jade's son was like: Jade gave so little away. 'What's he into?'

'No idea.' Jade roamed towards the recipe books and found one on traditional country fare. 'I mean, I know what he's into, but I've no idea what I'm hunting for. This looks nice. Is it local?'

'Yes, and very authentic. A bit too authentic, perhaps. I've had it for a while.'

Jade flicked through the pages and pulled a face. 'Blood pudding? Ew. Tansy? What's tansy? Nah.' She replaced the book and picked up another on old English drinks. 'Wassail? That's a sort of punch, isn't it? Christmassy?'

'Older than Christmas.'

'Mmm. That might do, but then . . . I wouldn't have a cauldron big enough, and the ingredients… Would I need a liquor licence?' she muttered. 'Yes, I would. Drat, too late to get one of those, and probably not a good idea. Too many kids in the shop.'

Wondering what on earth her friend was talking about, Fi left Jade to it and went to serve a woman with a pile of children's books and stocking fillers.

The shop was filling. Despite the sign asking them not to, people were bringing in hot drinks bought from Willow's Wagon, parked on the riverbank outside. Fi felt as if she needed eyes everywhere to be sure no one spilt anything. She went to help someone looking for an obscure title among the secondhand books as a gift for his brother, rescuing a half-empty paper cup from a display table and handing it to Nerys as she scuttled past.

Over the man's shoulder she could see Jade standing in the art section, picking books up and putting them down again. As she moved, the sparkles on her skirts flickered and changed. Perhaps Fi should hire her as a sort of Christmas light. It might be cheaper than electricity. She giggled to herself as she found an equivalent book and offered it to the customer.

As he turned its pages, Jade suddenly cried 'Brainwave! Photographs!' Tucking a couple of volumes from the art section under her arm, she rushed to the Christmas display, snatched the folklore book and dashed to the steps. 'Gotta dash!' she called over her shoulder. 'I'll text you and send the dosh!' In a flurry of black, purple and mirrored lights, she disappeared.

'Oh no!' said the customer with the old book. 'Shoplifter?'

Fi shook her head. 'Business buddy. No idea what she's up to this time. She's often a bit unpredictable.'

'Ah,' said the customer, with a smile. 'A mad friend. Everyone needs one of those. Life's very dull without them.'

'Rrrerrfff!' agreed Stan.

CHAPTER 3

Jade shifted from foot to foot on the station platform, her hands jammed in her pockets. She glanced at the display above her head, which informed her that the train, due twenty minutes ago, was expected in three minutes. 'If I'd known it would be this late…' she grumbled, peering down the track, though the train was too far away to see.

Would that make a good photo, I wonder? She took her phone from her bag, opened the camera app and zoomed in until her screen showed the track receding into the distance, surrounded by greenery, with a sky of palest blue. She clicked and inspected the picture. It was slightly crooked. *Could probably straighten that*, she thought, and held her phone up for another go.

As she did, a tiny speck of light appeared in the middle of the screen and began to grow. She took another picture, then put her phone in her pocket. *About time too.*

Finally, the train shuddered to a halt. Everyone else on the platform, which amounted to a woman towing a toddler, an elderly man with a newspaper under his arm, and a woman wearing a skirt suit and ridiculous heels, moved towards it. Jade hung back, not wishing to get caught up in the fray as they tried to get on while others tried to get off.

In the end only a few people disembarked, but Hugo was not among them. *Don't tell me he's not on here, after all that. I could have stayed in the shop. Or gone out and taken more photos.*

Since she had devised her festive money-making idea, Jade had roamed Hazeby-on-Wyvern looking for atmospheric scenes to take pictures of. She longed for a beautiful sunrise over the hills in which the town nestled. A dramatic sunset would be good, too. And snow would be the icing on the cake. The weather had been uncooperative, though, offering her grey skies and mizzle.

But tomorrow, if all went well, that would change.

She heard a whistle, and sighed. The next train wasn't due for at least another hour.

Suddenly a door opened and Hugo emerged, laden with a laptop bag and a large turquoise hard-shell wheelie case. He was wearing a tweed jacket with elbow patches and red corduroy trousers.

'Hugo!' Jade waved, then dashed towards him and enveloped him in a hug. 'I thought you'd missed the train.'

'Hello, Mummy. Gosh, you're like a boa constrictor.'

'Thanks.' She released him. 'How long are you staying for, a month?' She tapped the suitcase.

'I prefer to be prepared,' he replied. 'Are we walking?'

'No, the car's parked outside. Which is as well, looking at that beast. Let's get home, and I'll put the kettle on.'

Jade took Hugo through the station and into the car park.

'You've still got Bertha, then,' said Hugo, as they approached a medium-sized red Volvo with a small dent on the left front wing.

'Yup.' She opened the boot and Hugo heaved his luggage in. 'In you get. No, not in the back. I'm not your chauffeur.'

'Sorry, force of habit.' He grinned. 'Too used to taxis.'

Jade rolled her eyes and got behind the wheel. 'Poor Bertha hardly gets any exercise these days. It's ridiculous how much you can do online.' Bertha started on the second try.

'Isn't it,' said Hugo, as they moved slowly off. Their speed was less down to good driving habits than

Bertha's tendency to splutter to a halt if she wasn't handled gently. 'Automation software, AI, bots…'

'If you say so. Now, do you want to go straight home or shall I take you on a tour of the town?'

'Straight home, please,' Hugo said immediately. 'Then I can unpack and hopefully everything won't be too creased.'

'Oh. OK.'

'And I've got to be on a call at four.'

'I see.' Jade changed gear with some force and Bertha groaned.

'I know, Mummy, and I'm sorry. It was meant to be yesterday, but it got moved to today because there were server problems. Once it's done, though, that's it: I'll be free to play. Well, apart from keeping on top of emails and dealing with absolute emergencies. Not that I'm expecting any.'

'Can't someone else look after that?'

'Most things, yes, but you never know. Anyway, won't you be working in Candy Dreams?'

'Crystal Dreams, Hugo. And yes, but not all the time. I'm closing early on Christmas Eve and I won't reopen until, oh, not until the twenty-seventh at least. And Netta will be there, too.' She paused. 'I can imagine you on the phone to someone in Los Angeles, cutting a deal while I'm carving the turkey.'

'That's a bit harsh,' said Hugo, and she could tell from his tone that he was rattled.

She sighed. 'Sorry. It's just that I don't see you that often.'

'It's not exactly an easy trip,' said Hugo. 'Not by public transport.'

'You still haven't got a car, then.'

'Better for the environment.'

'You could get an electric one.'

'Or I could hire one,' said Hugo. 'Or join a car club. But I don't really need one, not in Oxford.'

Jade turned into a back street, took a left, and parked Bertha beside a small patch of waste ground, between a black Mini and a yellow Citroen 2CV.

'I'm confused,' said Hugo, gazing around him.

'The shop doesn't come with a parking space,' said Jade. 'No one minds if I park here, it's free, and I can see Bertha out of the upstairs window.'

He shrugged. 'Fair enough.'

They walked together, Jade telling Hugo various things about the town. She had to raise her voice to make herself heard over the noise of the wheeled suitcase.

They entered the high street. 'The shop's just down there.' She pointed. 'Do you want to take a peek downstairs? You could say hello to Netta.'

Hugo checked his watch. It looked very simple, which made Jade suspect it was expensive. 'I've got that call.'

'Course you have.' Jade held in a huff. 'Right,

come on then.' She unlocked the bottom door and held it open.

'Thanks, Mummy.' For such a beanpole, he managed the suitcase easily up the stairs. Jade followed, and he stood aside to let her open the flat door.

'Home sweet home,' she said, and ushered him in.

A grey day didn't suit the flat. It made the walls dingy, and the slightly wonky furniture cast strange shadows. Jade watched Hugo survey the main living area. He was smiling, but she couldn't read his face at all. She'd found that hard ever since he'd been a small boy.

'Cup of tea?' she asked.

He turned. 'Have you got decaf?'

Jade couldn't hold the huff in any longer. 'I haven't. I'll get some.'

'You don't have to. Water is fine.'

'OK. If you want to unpack, I've made room on the left-hand side of my wardrobe. Bedroom's through there.' She pointed. 'I'm afraid you're on the sofa.'

'That's fine. Ugh, the time! All right if I park myself here?' He sat down in the middle of the sofa and unzipped his laptop bag. He set a slim matt-black laptop on the coffee table, followed by various cables, a notebook, and a silver pen. Finally, he unzipped another pocket and brought out what looked like a flat white plastic doughnut on a tripod.

‘What on earth is that?’ asked Jade.

‘Portable ring light,’ said Hugo.

‘Well I never.’

‘It’s solar powered.’

‘I daresay. What does it do?’

‘It’s flattering. People use them on videos and things.’ He fussed with the laptop, plugging in various bits and bobs. ‘I’m assuming you don’t have super-fast broadband.’

Jade snorted. ‘You assume correctly.’

He looked up. ‘Mummy, you don’t have to stick around if you’d rather not. You’d probably find it boring.’

‘Possibly,’ said Jade. ‘OK, I’ll get you that water then head to the shop. How long will you be?’

‘An hour. Ish.’ Hugo considered. ‘Maybe an hour and a half?’

‘I’ll go downstairs.’

***

Jade headed up at five past five and heard Hugo say something about leverage. She shook her head and retreated.

At twenty to six, he was still talking. *I suppose I’m getting some exercise*, thought Jade, as she descended.

‘Hasn’t he finished yet?’ said Netta.

‘Nope. Why don’t you head home, Netta? I know I said we’d stay open until six, but I didn’t expect to be at a loose end once Hugo got here.'

'I was just going to neaten that display,' said Netta.

'I'll still pay you till six.'

Netta immediately left the counter and took her coat off its hook. 'I'll see you tomorrow.' She shrugged her way into her coat, then took a cream bobble hat out of her pocket and pulled it over her long, dark hair. 'Maybe I'll get to see Hugo, too.'

'I'll drag him downstairs, never fear. Anyway, make sure you get plenty of sleep. Big day tomorrow.'

Netta looked mystified for a moment, then her face cleared. 'Oh yes, the winter solstice.'

'Yes,' said Jade. 'I'm hoping I'll be able to offer people something special.'

'What's that?'

Jade grinned. 'Tell you tomorrow.'

***

After cashing up, Jade climbed the stairs to the flat once more. She could no longer hear Hugo's voice. She opened the door. 'All done?'

She was just in time to see Hugo shove something under a cushion. 'Yes, we've finished,' he said.

'Good stuff. Fi's invited us for a drink at her boat – her family are visiting – and then I thought we could eat out. The Vine is nice, or the Duck and Druid. But I imagine you want to unpack first.'

'Please.' He stood and stretched. 'Oof. I feel as if I've been sitting in the same position for hours.'

'You have, for at least two,' said Jade. 'Why don't you get a shower?'

'I might, actually.' He lowered his arms. 'What time do you want to eat?'

'Early. I'm getting up at stupid o'clock tomorrow morning.'

'Are you? Why?'

Jade considered how much to tell him. 'I'm visiting Hazeby Stone Circle. It's the winter solstice, and I'm hoping to catch the sunrise over the stones.'

Hugo gave her an incredulous look. 'You won't be wearing a long robe and chanting, will you, Mummy?'

'Don't be ridiculous,' said Jade. 'If you must know, I'm planning to take photographs and sell them in the shop. A sort of Christmas exclusive. Rick next door will frame them.' Not that she'd got round to asking him yet, but she was sure he would.

'Whatever floats your boat,' said Hugo, and laughed. 'Or that of your customers.' He thought for a moment. 'What camera are you using?'

'Phone.' Jade held it up.

'Oh. If you wanted, you could borrow my phone. It has four cameras and absolutely tons of megapixels.'

'I'll stick to what I know, thanks.'

'I could come too. We could take a breakfast picnic, make it a proper outing. Hard-boiled eggs and smashed avocado on artisan bread.'

What on earth has he been reading? 'That sounds

like a recipe for indigestion. And you, out before dawn? I'll believe it when I see it.'

Hugo drew himself up. 'Some of us have early meetings these days.'

'Maybe. But I've only got one shot at this, and I'd rather not have to chivvy you out of bed first. Chivvying myself will be bad enough. I can't stay long anyway, because we'll be opening at nine on the dot.'

'Fine, Mummy.' Hugo seized the handle of his wheelie case, trundled it into the bedroom, and closed the door.

Jade glared at it. *Kids*. She moved quietly to the sofa and lifted the cushion. Underneath was Hugo's phone.

She picked it up. On the lockscreen was an alert from Airbnb. *Re: apartment with roof terrace in Hazeby*.

Slowly, Jade replaced the phone under the cushion. It looked like being a long few days.

CHAPTER 9

The day before midwinter might be dark by four pm, but at least it was dry. Closing the Book Barge early, Fi put the canopy up on deck with her son Dylan's help, providing a comfortable outdoor space for her parents and in-laws. From the deck they could see the town, sparkling with Christmas lights and ablaze with colour.

They'd strung extra lights of their own inside the canopy, and by the time the family arrived at three it looked cosy and festive. The heater provided enough warmth for Fi's mother-in-law Annie to remove her scarf, though she chatted to Fi's mother with her hands clasped round her mug of tea as if it were a chalice full of life-sustaining elixir. *Then again, that's how tea drinkers always think of tea,* thought Fi, and chuckled quietly.

She sat in the corner and contemplated her family.

Dylan was showing his grandmothers some photos on his phone, from his visit to a film set. He'd spent several hours acting for what would no doubt be edited down to five minutes of fame when the programme aired. Fi's father-in-law Nigel had Stan on his lap and was feeding him treats. Fi's father was below, communing with the books and mulling wine.

Fi looked at the sky, trying to work out what its intentions were. *Call yourself a seafarer.* The memory of Marcus's message made her smile. *I bet he can read clouds. Perhaps I should send him a photo and ask if the mizzle is likely to keep off, so the canopy won't have to be stored away damp.*

A gust of wind fluttered the canvas and blew Annie's scarf onto the deck.

'Batten down the hatches!' cried Nigel. 'If the wind gets under the canopy it might lift the whole boat and carry her to the Netherlands.'

'France would be better,' said Fi's mother.

'The prevailing wind is wrong, Trisha,' said Nigel, as if the possibility of *Coralie* sailing through the air was simply a matter of geography, not physics.

'Perhaps, but there are some perfect places near us in Normandy where Fi could moor *Coralie* and run the same enterprise.' There was a determined, organising glint in Fi's mother's eye, tempered with wistfulness.

'I'm sure the French have bookshops covered,

Mum,' said Fi. 'I doubt they'd want me muscling in.'

'You'd be selling books in English for the tourist and expat market,' argued her mother. 'You could have a little *salon du thé* on board. And the weather would be more reliable. I've been meaning to suggest it for when Dylan's finished his A levels. You've two and a half years to plan. It would be lovely.'

'Cool!' said Dylan. 'When I'm at uni or drama school, I can say I have a property in France.'

Fi watched Annie's expression flicker between mutinous and panic-stricken. In Annie's view, living an hour's drive from Dylan was bad enough. To have her grandson potentially based in another country would be something else again. She looked as if she might cry.

'Don't count your chickens, Dylan,' said Fi. 'You've got to get your GCSEs first, and even if I went for what Grandma's suggesting, you'd probably want to stay in the UK some of the time. I'm sure Nana would be happy to have you visit.' *Or more likely, you won't want any of us. You'll be hanging out with friends or travelling the world.* The sudden realisation that her son was on the verge of adulthood made her own eyes prickle with tears. *How does Jade manage when she barely sees Hugo? Why do they seem so distant from each other? Did something happen? Will Dylan and I end up the same?*

Dylan, oblivious to the emotions of his female

relations, shrugged. 'Don't talk about GCSEs, Mum, I'm still recovering from the mocks.' He checked his phone. 'Aargh, look at the time! Gotta get to the theatre.' He jumped to his feet. 'Safe journey to Nana's, see you on Christmas Day!' He kissed his grandmothers and rushed down the gangplank.

'You've forgotten your coat!' yelled Annie and Fi's mother simultaneously, but he'd been swallowed by the darkness.

'I'm surprised you let him help at the theatre after . . . you know,' said Annie, settling back in her chair with a slight frown.

'That was a one-off,' said Fi. 'And he's always helped in the Christmas pantomime. This year, he's getting paid. In fact, after New Year he'll be working there every Saturday and Sunday afternoon.'

'You'll miss his help on the Book Barge,' said her mother. 'And you'll have to hire a replacement.'

'Zach will increase his hours and I won't be paying Dylan for that time,' said Fi, omitting the fact that she'd have to pay Zach more than she paid Dylan. 'I'll go and help Dad with the mulled wine and nibbles.'

'Pete hasn't forgotten a non-alcoholic version, has he?' asked Annie. 'Your mother is driving us back.'

'He won't have. Don't panic.'

Below deck, Fi found her father ensconced on the sofa, reading a 1970s copy of *The Little World of Don Camillo* and chuckling. Aromas of mulled wine wafted from the galley.

Fi sat on the sofa and leaned against him. He set the book down and put an arm round her shoulders. 'What's up, sweetheart?'

Fi sighed. 'Annie's not happy about Dylan working at the theatre. I haven't even told her that he and his mates are thinking of starting a rock band.' She pulled a face. 'I blame Jade's neighbour Rick for inspiring them.'

'Working in performing arts is all Dylan's ever wanted to do,' said her father. 'She'll have to get used to it.'

'I know,' said Fi. 'And then there's Mum. She wants me to move to France and run the Book Barge near you.'

'Does she? Just when I thought we'd finally got rid of you.'

Fi nudged him in the ribs.

Her father laughed and gave her shoulders a squeeze. 'Seriously, that would be lovely. For now, it's good to spend Christmas with you here. Or rather, at Annie's. It's good of her to put us up.'

'She's not complaining about my parenting too much, is she?'

'Not at all.' Another squeeze. 'She loves you very much, Fi. She just doesn't understand why you're doing what you're doing. Or, for that matter, why your mum and I retired early and started a gîte complex in

Normandy. Some of us are adventurous, while some prefer not to take risks. Annie wants you and Dylan to be secure.'

There was silence as they mulled this over. 'How are things, Fi?' said her father, eventually.

Fi twisted round to look at him. 'In what way?'

'These are hard times, financially. Your mum and I are just keeping our heads above water. Are you? If you're not, please say. Perhaps we can pool resources somehow. Sorry, I seem to keep using nautical analogies.'

'We're doing all right,' she said. 'I'd like a better profit margin, and I need to work out how to improve it next year, but at least there *is* a profit. It's always hard at this time of year. It's busy in the daytime, but there's no point being open after three in December because hardly anyone ventures down here in the dark. I only bother on Thursdays when it's late Christmas-shopping evening.'

'Fair enough.'

'It helps having Jade in the town – we can support and bounce ideas off each other. Though I'm not entirely convinced about her latest one. There's photography, and photography.'

'Pardon?' Fi's father's eyes widened. 'She's not going, um, exotic, is she?'

'No, Dad! Honestly! I'm talking midwinter landscapes!'

'Phew! You can't blame me for wondering, given all the excitement you've got yourself mixed up in ever since she came to town.'

'That's a coincidence. You like her.'

'I do,' said her father. 'I'm looking forward to chatting with her this evening; I think she's one of the best friends you've ever had. I'd just rather the two of you stuck to shopkeeping.'

'We'd prefer that, too.'

'May I ask . . . how's your love life?'

'Dad!' Fi protested, then shrugged. 'I had a near miss in the autumn, but you needn't worry about digging out my embarrassing baby photos.' Her phone, with its messages from Marcus, felt warm in her pocket. There weren't many, and they were nothing more than friendly, but…

'Dylan showed me this earlier.' Her father picked up a notebook from the arm of the sofa.

She knew it well: it was where Dylan jotted ideas for theatre sets. Fi suspected that ultimately he would end up in production rather than before the footlights, but left him to it, glad he wasn't always glued to a video game. She frowned. 'What does that have to do with me or my non-existent love life?'

'I wondered if the past was holding you back.'

'What?'

Fi's father turned the pages. Photographs, cuttings, and tickets shifted and he resettled them. Finally, he extracted a piece of newspaper which had once been screwed up then flattened out, and handed it to her.

Fi recognised it at once. It was the Italian article on a fishing competition that someone had sent her in October, including a photograph featuring a man who resembled her dead husband. She willed her hand not to shake. 'How odd. This was in the log basket months ago, ready to use as kindling.'

'Dylan must have taken it out,' said her father. 'Where did it come from?'

'Someone sent it to my old address because that person looks a bit like Gavin.' She pointed, but didn't touch the photo.

'Odd sense of humour.' Fi's father was the only person she'd told in detail about the financial mess Gavin had left behind when he'd abandoned her and Dylan. 'I can see why you'd throw it away.'

'I wonder why Dylan rescued it. Did he show it to you specifically?'

Fi's father shook his head. 'He was showing me sketches and ideas inspired by a drama lesson on *Commedia dell'arte* and it slipped out. I'm pretty sure it was in that section. I was worried you'd kept it because you were hankering after Gavin.'

'Hardly.'

'Good,' said her father. 'Maybe Dylan spotted the newspaper in the basket when he went to light the log burner and thought it might give him a feel for

Italian.'

'Ha,' said Fi. 'I bet you're right. There's probably a school trip in the offing he's forgotten to tell me about.'

'Maybe put the book in his cabin,' said her father. 'I'll rescue the mulled wine before it evaporates.' They stood up and he gave her a hug. 'I'm glad you're all right, sweetheart.'

'Thanks.' She hugged him back and he headed to the galley, singing 'Here I come a-wassailing!'

Fi slipped the cutting in the notebook and went into Dylan's cabin. As she looked for somewhere sensible to put the book among the chaos, a photograph fell out. She picked it up. It was of Gavin, taken at their wedding all those years ago. Another photo was working its way out, too. Knowing she shouldn't snoop, but unable to stop herself, Fi opened the notebook. The second photograph was of Gavin at Dylan's age. And instead of notes and drawings to do with the theatre or film sets, the page was filled with sketches of a child holding hands with a man, of two men – one older, one younger – chatting over beer, and a cutting from the memorial service they'd held for Gavin. The page was headed *Father and son – if only*.

Poor Dylan. It really was time she talked to him about it. If nothing else, there would be plenty of time at Christmas.

CHAPTER 5

At twenty past six, tired of checking her phone every few minutes, Jade threw off the bedcovers and got up. She was too twitchy to rest, anyway. Her alarm was set for half past six, which would give her plenty of time, but she didn't particularly want it to go off and wake Hugo.

She had laid out her clothes ready at the foot of the bed – a pair of jeans, a T-shirt and a jumper, along with the thickest socks she owned. She crept towards them in the darkness and stubbed her toe on the bed leg. 'Ow!'

She bit back a swearword and froze, listening, then edged round the bed and felt for her clothes.

'Mummy, is that you?'

Jade allowed herself a sigh. 'Yes, Hugo. Go back to sleep.' *I never thought I'd have to say that again.* Hugo had been one of those babies who seemed to need relatively little sleep: good humoured, but lively. Exhausting, in other words.

'It's really early.'

'Yes. That's the point. As I said yesterday.'

'Are you sure you don't want me to come with you?'

'I'll be fine,' Jade said, through gritted teeth.

'Should you be heading into the middle of nowhere when it's pitch black outside?'

'Hugo, this is a sleepy market town. I wouldn't have thought that Oxford was rife with crime, apart from in *Inspector Morse*, but round here is safe.'

She heard a creak. 'Apart from those two murders you were mixed up in.'

'That was different. Anyway, I must get going or I'll miss the sunrise.' Jade put her bedside light on, since she didn't have to worry about waking Hugo any more, and scrambled into her clothes.

When she opened her bedroom door, Hugo was sitting on the sofa in a pair of red and blue paisley pyjamas and a bottle-green dressing gown in what appeared to be satin and velvet. A paisley eye mask pushed onto his forehead completed the ensemble. 'Shall I make you a flask of tea?' he asked.

'Thanks for the offer, but I don't think there's time.'

Hugo glanced at his phone. 'Sunrise isn't till eight or so. I checked.'

‘So did I,’ said Jade, fetching her Doc Martens from their place by the door and sitting beside him on the sofa. ‘But I don’t know when first light is. It might be earlier. Anyway, I’ve got to drive there, get to the circle and settle in.’ She eased her left foot into her boot and began to lace it.

‘Well, I hope it goes brilliantly,’ said Hugo. ‘Don’t forget what I said about photo editing. There are some good apps, or you could get a free trial of Photoshop. And you need high-quality paper for printing—’

‘I’m aware of that. But if I don’t get a move on I won’t have a photograph to edit, much less print.’ She put on her right boot and laced it, then went to the bathroom.

When she returned, Hugo was reading something on his phone. He put it aside when he saw her. ‘Are you going now, Mummy? Make sure you text me when you get there, and again when you’ve finished.’

‘Yes, sir.’ Jade clicked her heels together and saluted.

Hugo gave her a reproachful look. ‘I just want to make sure you’re safe.’

‘I know,’ said Jade. ‘But I’m used to being my own person and not having to check in. And yes, I’ll text.’ She leaned over and kissed him on the forehead, above the sleeping mask. ‘I’ll see you in an hour and a half or so.’

‘Bye, Mummy. Good luck with the photos.’ He

stretched himself out on the sofa and put his hands behind his head.

Jade crept downstairs, let herself out, and picked her way through the dark streets towards Bertha. The pavement was slightly slippery beneath her feet, while the air was dry and chilly, and she hoped that would make for an atmospheric, frosty scene at the stone circle. *Grass as sharp as blades of ice, and lurking mist.* She puffed out her own dragon breath as she walked.

Bertha took a few goes to start. 'I don't blame you,' Jade told her, as she waited a few seconds before turning the key again. 'It is a bit early for adventures.'

Bertha coughed. Once, twice more, then the engine caught. 'There we go.'

The roads were quiet, with an occasional car moving stealthily along. As she drove, Jade saw lights on here and there in the houses she passed, but most of Hazeby-on-Wyvern seemed to be tucked up in bed. *Trust you, Jade*, she thought. *Up with the lark, on another one of your daft schemes.*

A business enterprise, she told herself, and took the road that led to the stone circle.

The circle was about a mile and a half out of town. Jade had seen pictures of it on the web, but had never visited. She had checked beforehand that there was a free car park, though, and that the site was always open. She hummed to the radio she had put on low for a bit of company, looking for her turning, and almost missed it when a large lorry thundered past her. Luckily, she managed to brake in time.

The road was narrow and winding, with passing places every so often, a high sloping hedge on either side, and no street lights. Jade drove carefully, hoping she wouldn't meet any fast local drivers coming the other way.

After a couple of minutes, she saw a sign: white letters on a green background. *HAZEBY STONE CIRCLE CAR PARK*, with an arrow.

Jade drove Bertha into a small gravelled area and parked near the noticeboard. She got out, moving carefully on the pitted surface, and inspected the board by the light of her phone torch.

A laminated map was pinned to the board, with *You Are Here* and a red-dotted route to the stone circle through what looked like a field. Underneath was a notice:

The distance from this car park to the stone circle is approximately 500 metres. The route is level, but sensible footwear is recommended.

Much of the pathway to the stone circle is a public right-of-way through a farm. Please respect this by keeping to the path and taking any litter home with you. Please keep dogs on a lead.

'Right. Off we go, I suppose.' She locked Bertha, stamped her feet on the gravel a couple of times, angled her phone so that it illuminated the path, and set out.

More than once, as Jade walked, she wished that she had let Hugo come with her. It wasn't as if she was scared: of course not. But it was very quiet, apart from an occasional rustle. Once, an owl hooted, and Jade nearly jumped out of her skin. She paused for a moment to catch her breath, then continued. *The return journey will be easier*, she told herself as she moved gingerly along. *The sun will be up and I'll be able to see where I'm going. It can't be much further.*

On she walked, occasionally stumbling at a ridge or a hollow. How big could one field be? *I wonder what grows here*, she thought, to keep her mind occupied. *Potatoes, broccoli, carrots…* Listing all the vegetables she could think of, including some she'd never encountered in real life, used a bit more time.

At long last, her phone picked out a fence ahead. 'Thank heavens,' said Jade, and plodded towards it. She glanced at the sky. Was it a little lighter? She quickened her pace.

The path led to a stile – of course – and though she wanted to hurry, Jade took her time climbing over, testing each step before putting her weight on it. The last thing she wanted was to have to hobble to the car on a twisted ankle. Apart from anything else, Hugo would never let her hear the end of it. She imagined him shaking his head at her folly with an 'Oh dear,

Mummy' and an indulgent smile, and gritted her teeth.

When at last she was on firm ground again, a large and slightly more professional sign said *STONE CIRCLE THIS WAY*. Jade shone her phone in the direction of the arrow, and there they were. The stones, perhaps thirty metres away. They loomed over the meadow in which they were set, and just as she had hoped, a low mist hovered above the grass. Gaps showed here and there, but it was impressive enough to make Jade catch her breath. Surely it would be even more impressive at first light.

'Excellent,' said Jade, and giggled at the plume of smoke the word created. *Steady on. Don't get light-headed, not all on your own out here.*

She walked down the path until she reached an information board with a labelled line drawing of the stones. The one in the middle was an altar, apparently. *Must get that dead centre*, thought Jade.

She leaned on the board for stability and focused her phone camera on the stones. Perhaps a wide shot, showing the stones against a background of rolling hills, then a close-up or two? Hopefully the mist wouldn't dissolve too quickly.

She zoomed in to see if it was still there—

What's that?

Something was lying on top of the altar stone. Jade sighed. Probably someone's jacket or a plastic bag full of litter. *Stupid tourists, or picnickers.* She hurried down the path to remove it, cursing them under her breath. But as she got closer she realised that whatever it was was too big to be a jacket. She lifted her phone light—

'Oh my God.' She stopped dead, and nearly dropped the phone. 'It can't be.'

For a moment, she considered leaving. Crossing the field, driving home in Bertha, and telling Hugo that in the end she'd got cold feet. Metaphorically, that was.

People will wonder what you were doing here.

They'll ask questions.

They'll probably be suspicious. Scratch that: they will be suspicious.

But even as she thought it, she knew she couldn't turn her back on what she had seen.

She walked forward, holding her phone out to light the way.

On the stone altar lay a body. It appeared to be naked, but as she drew closer she saw that it wore a pair of underpants. The body was that of a man, thin enough for his ribs to show, but the face was horribly bruised, with swollen black eyes, and covered in cuts. The man's chest didn't seem to be moving, and when Jade held a trembling hand above the mouth, she felt no breath.

You could still run.

Jade looked back to the fence in the distance.

He might not be dead.

Jade gripped her phone tightly and pressed *Emergency Call.*

'Which service do you require?' said the calm voice at the other end.

Jade took a deep breath. 'Police and possibly ambulance. I hope so. I'm at Hazeby Stone Circle and I've found a body.'

CHAPTER 6

Fi woke with a start at ten to seven. She lay blinking in the dark cabin, calming herself by listening to the river. *It's midwinter day. That's why I've woken early. My mind wants to say goodbye to the gloom. No, that's not it. It's the thought of talking to Dylan about his dad today.* She let out a tiny groan, then realised it was something else: a sixth sense making her uneasy.

The alarm on her phone went off as a call came in, and the vibrating phone shimmied its way towards the edge of her bedside table.

'Oh no you don't.' She caught it, stopped the alarm and looked at the display. *Jade?* Jade couldn't function before eight at the earliest, and was barely coherent until she'd had three cups of tea.

'Hello? What's wrong?'

Jade's words rattled out at the speed of machine gun bullets. 'Battery's really low. Why does this happen to me all the time? It's terrible… Should I cover him? . . . Just underpants… Ought to be funny but it's not… Can you help?'

Definitely not coherent until she'd had enough tea.

'Slow down, Jade,' said Fi. 'Plug the phone in. I don't want to know what Hugo wears to bed. If he needs a blanket, can't he get his own?'

'I'm not at home. No socket… There's a dead man.'

Fi was fully awake now. She put her bedside light on, as if that would help make sense of things. 'What man? Where are you?'

'A stranger. Hazeby Stone Circle.'

'The stone circle? Wh—'

'Please come.'

'Have you rung—'

'Yes. But I'm alone… Just hurry! It's dark out here. My ba—' The phone went dead.

Fi washed quickly, shivered her way into warm clothes, grabbed a torch, a portable phone charger and a couple of cables, and stuffed them in a backpack with her purse.

Stan looked up sleepily from his basket in the kitchen and wagged his tail. 'Sorry, you can't come,' she told him. She knocked on Dylan's cabin door. 'If I'm not back by eight thirty, can you take Stan for a walk and open up for Zach?'

'Aw Muuum, it's the holidays!'

'Not for me it isn't. Hopefully I won't be that long.'

It's already gone seven o'clock. She left the boat, locking the wheelhouse door behind her, crossed the barely visible, dew-slippery gangplank, then rushed across the dark meadows to the car park. At least there was no frost to scrape off the windows.

Even on high beam, the car lights were barely capable of illuminating the road. Hedges and trees lurked in a midwinter gloom that seemed to be increasing, not fading. Fi drove as fast as she could, periodically blinded by cars and trucks coming the other way. She'd only ever been to the stones once, on a bright summer afternoon, but they'd made her shiver despite the sunshine. Not a rational response, but real all the same.

They always say the darkest hour is just before dawn, she told herself. *It's nothing to do with standing stones creeping me out, or whatever Jade's found.*

Finally, she saw the turning. Her car bumped over the rutted lane till she parked next to Jade's car, which was on its own. Perhaps Jade hadn't rung for help because she wanted Fi's advice first, but surely she'd have more sense than that.

Fi got out of the car, switched on the torch and hurried along the path until she reached the stones. She flashed her torch around. She couldn't see Jade: just a shape on what locals called the altar. Then a dark something moved forwards. Irrationally, Fi felt the urge to back away and run. 'Jade?' Her voice wobbled.

'Thank goodness.' Jade's voice was shaky too. 'I thought you were never coming.'

'I came as quickly as I could.' Fi hugged her.

Jade shivered in her arms. She didn't have a coat on, and her thick woollen sweater was dewy. 'My phone's dead and I can't see my watch, so I didn't know the time. I felt as if I'd entered another dimension.'

'Here's a battery,' said Fi, letting go of Jade to rummage in her backpack. 'I brought all the leads I have; hopefully one fits. Why didn't you wait in your car?'

'Didn't want to stay with *him*.' Jade looked towards the stones. 'But I couldn't leave him, either. I think someone beat him up and left him there to die.'

'Oh.'

'It didn't seem respectful, especially as he's practically naked. I put my coat over him in case he is still alive. I read once that no one's dead until they're warm and dead.'

Fi stared at her. 'What?'

'Someone who had hypothermia went into a coma so deep that they couldn't detect any life, but they came to at room temperature, so to speak.'

'Right.' Fi grimaced, wondering if the story had

been part of some weird research for Jade's shop. 'You've called an ambulance?'

'And the police. Will you come and take a look?'

Fi shuddered. 'All right. Take my coat, or we'll be testing that hypothermia theory on you.'

'Yes, Mum.'

'Stop rolling your eyes.'

'How do you know I am?'

'I can hear them.'

Jade managed a half-hearted chuckle as she put Fi's coat over her shoulders and they trudged towards the stones.

In the torchlight, the chiselled menhirs seemed to be leaning forwards, as if to see them better. Fi wished she could remember whether the circle was supposed to be friendly or malevolent. Currently the stones appeared curious, like bystanders at the aftermath of a collision. 'What exactly were you doing here at ungodly o'clock?' she asked.

'I wanted to take photos of the sun rising behind the stones.'

'It's not like you to commune with nature.'

'I was planning to print the pictures and sell them – mystic midwinter photos for the shop.'

'Really?' Fi shone the torch around. Jade had only bought a book on photography the other day. That wasn't long enough to pick up the necessary skills, unless she was brushing up on something she already knew. 'Where's your camera and tripod? And your filters, to cope with the exposure and light contrast and all that stuff?'

'I was going to take the pictures on my phone.'

'The one with the flat battery?' Fi asked, as they neared the covered figure on the altar stone.

'I forgot to bring a torch, so I used the battery walking here then phoning emergency services.' Jade looked wretched. Now probably wasn't the time to question her photographic skills. 'Do you know how to tell if someone's dead?'

'No,' said Fi. 'But if you hold the torch, I can try.' She hugged herself as she approached the body. The sky beyond him was a fraction less black.

Jade's coat covered the man from head to knees. His feet pointed upwards in rather a ridiculous manner. Their colour suggested they were colder than the stone on which he lay.

Fi lifted the coat from the man's head and shoulders. A long time ago, she'd seen her grandfather's body in his coffin after a peaceful death. He had seemed waxen, unreal. Every spark of personality was gone, leaving just a shell. This stranger, despite the bruises and injuries, had a similar appearance. Otherwise, Fi had no idea what to look for and racked her brain for what little knowledge she'd gained from novels and television shows.

It was hard to be certain, but the man's face and

chest seemed paler than what she could see of his back. Could that be lividity: gravity's effect on blood which was no longer being pumped around a body? Gently, she touched the man's wounded cheek. It was colder than the air, and his slightly open jaw felt hard. His shoulder was rigid.

'I don't think he'll come round, Jade,' she said. 'I can't swear to it, but I'm pretty certain he's dead.'

She replaced the coat and blinked as something shiny caught the corner of her eye. She turned, and saw lights bobbing in the distance. For a moment, Fi wondered what on earth had happened to the sunrise, then realised she was looking the wrong way and the lights were too small. Two lights meant two people, at least, and the bobbing meant they were crossing the stile. 'Either the druids have arrived to do whatever druids do,' she said, 'or the emergency services are here.'

'Ms Fitch?' A man and woman in just-discernible green overalls approached, the woman carrying a large bag.

'That's me,' said Jade.

'We're paramedics,' said the man. 'I'm Bob, this is Karen. Are you all right? Karen can check you for shock. Was the casualty known to you?'

'No, he wasn't. I'm OK, thanks.'

'Where's the casualty?'

'Over there, on the altar.' Jade pointed. 'I was out

for a walk and found him.'

'With a coat over him?'

'No, that's mine,' said Jade. 'I covered him, just in case… I don't want it back.'

'Righto.' The paramedics took their equipment to the stone altar and carefully lifted the coat. After a few seconds, Bob replaced the coat. 'Here come the police.'

Another torch approached, and a woman in a long coat passed Fi and Jade as if they weren't there. 'I'm Inspector Acaster from Wyvernshire HQ, covering for Inspector Falconer,' she said to the paramedics. 'Any signs of life?'

'None,' said Karen.

'I'd say he's been dead some hours,' said Bob. 'How long exactly is for the coroner to determine. You're the expert, but it doesn't look natural to me.'

'Is that his coat?'

'No,' said Jade. 'It's mine. I didn't touch anything. I put it over him because—'

'There's no place for sentiment at a crime scene,' said Inspector Acaster. 'Are you the person who called it in?' She peered at her phone. 'Ms Jade Fitch?'

'Yes.'

She turned to Fi. 'And you are?'

'Ms Fi Booker.' Fi wished she could message Marcus before he heard another way. He'd be worried for them. For her.

'Wait a moment,' said Inspector Acaster. It was hard to make out her expression, but her voice sounded as if she was frowning. 'Ms Fitch and Ms Booker? I recognise those names. Inspector Falconer told me about you a while ago.'

'Oh good,' said Jade, brightening a little.

'You think so?' said Inspector Acaster. 'Perhaps you should think again.'

CHAPTER 7

This is what you get for doing the right thing, thought Jade. *You could have run for it and let someone else find the body, but no. You had to be a good girl and phone the police. And look where it's got you.*

'I didn't have to phone this in,' she said, before she could stop herself. 'I could have gone home.'

'You could,' said Inspector Acaster.

The sky was definitely beginning to lighten. It was a sort of mid-grey, shading to deep pink over the hills. Jade felt a pang of regret for the photographs that might have been, then brought herself back to the current situation. 'So it's good that I stayed and made the call, right?'

Inspector Acaster considered this. In the growing light she appeared to be in her late thirties, with cropped blonde hair which fell over one cynical eye. Jade wondered if she modelled herself on Kate

Fleming in *Line of Duty*. 'Possibly,' she said, at last.

Jade's eyes widened and she moved forward, but Fi grabbed her arm. 'Jade, you might be in shock. You should go home, or I can take you. You probably shouldn't drive.'

'Not just yet,' said Inspector Acaster. 'It's best to get first impressions. Besides, aren't you two dying to share your insights about the murder with me?' She studied them. 'Is that how it works? Or are you planning to keep the glory for yourselves?'

'That's uncalled for,' said Fi, and Jade shot her a surprised glance. 'Yes, we've assisted with solving a couple of local crimes, but we don't go looking for bodies.'

'Really?' said Inspector Acaster. 'I'm sure Marcus Falconer has been Mr Softly Softly Nice Guy as usual, but some of us think civilians who interfere in investigations are deeply suspect.'

'Didn't you say that you're filling in for him?' asked Fi.

The inspector pulled a notebook from her pocket. 'Tell me what happened.' She extracted the pen from its band and clicked it on. Even in the half light, Jade could see a distinct glint in her eye. 'What were you doing here, Ms Fitch? You don't have a dog with you, which is the usual reason for being out so early, and you're not in running gear. Please explain.'

Fi turned to the inspector. 'Surely you don't plan to

interrogate us in the middle of a field?'

'It's not an interrogation, Ms Booker, but as I say, early impressions can be useful, before imagination takes over. Ms Fitch, why did you come here? This isn't the sort of place you can go to on your way somewhere else.'

'I was…' Jade paused, aware how ridiculous her explanation would sound. *Could you invent something more plausible?* But racking her brains brought nothing to the surface.

Inspector Acaster laughed. 'Come on. Surely you know why you're here?'

'Couldn't Jade make a formal statement later?'

'Ms Booker, I want Ms Fitch's first impressions before things get embellished, in case she saw anything pertinent. Could you stand over there and leave me to ask the questions?' Ice lurked beneath the polite veneer of Inspector Acaster's question, but Fi didn't move.

'I came to take photographs,' blurted Jade. 'For the winter solstice. I run a crystal and magic shop, and I thought it was something my customers would appreciate.' Now it was out, she felt better.

The inspector stared at her with frank incredulity. 'At this time of day?'

'I was waiting for the sun to come up. Sunrise over the stone circle at the winter solstice.'

The inspector narrowed her eyes and gazed at the

horizon, where the pink tinge was growing stronger. 'Is that some sort of pagan thing? Witchcraft, and such?'

'It's a spiritual thing,' Jade said firmly. 'New beginnings.'

Inspector Acaster wrote a note. 'Really?'

'Jade told me about it,' said Fi. 'I think it's a great idea. Her customers will – would have loved it.'

They would, Jade thought sadly, as an orange glow illuminated the underside of a pale-grey cloud.

'I'm not sure the testimony of a close friend is worth much in the circumstances,' said Inspector Acaster. 'Especially that of a partner in crime, one might say.' She held up her pen as Fi opened her mouth, and addressed Jade again. 'So you were . . . taking photographs. On your phone?'

'Yes,' said Jade.

'Can you show me?'

'It was too dark to take any,' said Jade. She could feel her cheeks burning, and hoped it was too dark for the police officer to notice. 'But I've taken a lot of pictures round Hazeby lately. I can show you—'

'That won't be necessary. Tell me what happened, Ms Fitch, in your own words.'

Who else's words would I use? thought Jade. 'I left my flat at about half past six,' she said. 'My son can confirm that.'

'Your son?'

'Yes. He's staying with me over Christmas.'

'And his name is?'

'Hugo Fitch. Well, his name's Jack, but he calls himself Hugo.'

'Son uses an alias,' Inspector Acaster murmured as she wrote. 'Go on.'

'It isn't an alias,' said Jade. 'My son just prefers to be called Hugo. He isn't a criminal, if that's what you think.'

'Please go on.'

Oh, Hugo, I'm sorry for getting you caught up in this. Jade took a deep breath. 'I drove to the stone circle car park and walked across the field. That took a while, because it was so dark.'

'Yes,' said the inspector. 'Why did you leave so early? Presumably you know approximately when the sun rises at this time of year.'

'I Googled the time for sunrise today, obviously. But I thought it might start getting light before that, and I didn't want to miss it.'

'Right. Witness very early on scene.' She wrote another note. 'Continue, please.'

'I came to the stone circle and leaned on that information board to take pictures. I zoomed in on the stones, and that was when I spotted something on the altar.' She waited for Inspector Acaster to make another biting comment, but none was forthcoming. 'I thought it was litter or a coat that someone had left behind, so I went to move it. That was when I realised it was a body. I checked for breathing and found none. Then I called emergency services.'

'Mm-hm.' Inspector Acaster finished writing. 'At what time did you call your friend?'

'Just after I rang the emergency services. My battery was running low, and I was—' Jade swallowed. 'I was scared.'

'Definitely after, you say. Not before?'

Jade lifted her chin. 'I rang for police and an ambulance first, then I rang Fi.'

Inspector Acaster held out her hand. 'May I see your phone?'

Jade studied her feet. 'The battery's flat.'

'The battery . . . is flat,' said the inspector, in a tone that would have withered the hardiest of plants. 'You are telling me, Ms Fitch, that you came on an expedition which depended on your phone, and yet you had so little charge on it that the battery ran out.'

'I didn't know how much charge the torch would use,' said Jade. 'I haven't been here before. I didn't think I'd need it.'

'I suppose stupidity isn't a crime,' the inspector said meditatively. 'Did you touch the body, Ms Fitch?'

'No,' said Jade.

'Sure?'

'Yes. I was close to the body, but I never touched it. I put my coat over it in respect, and just in case he was still alive.'

Inspector Acaster turned to Fi. 'Did you touch it?'

'Yes,' said Fi. 'I checked the body for rigor mortis. I touched the cheek and the shoulder.'

The inspector's lip curled in a half-smile. 'That's very specific.'

'I don't think recognising death is particularly specialist.'

'Of course: that man was poisoned on your barge. By a book. And your barge happens to be a bookshop.' She gazed at the sunrise, brilliant in orange and pink, with purple shadows beneath the clouds. 'It's a nice day to take photos, I suppose.' She snapped her notebook shut and faced them. 'Could you both wait by the information board, in case I have any more questions. Some of us have a job to do.'

'Are you all right?' Fi whispered as they walked to the board.

'I've been better. You?'

'Likewise.'

Inspector Acaster took a pair of gloves from her pocket and put them on, then dropped to a crouch. 'Pile of clothes by the body,' she said. 'Men's clothes, folded neatly.' She stood up and inspected the body. 'Approximately the right size, but hard to tell without unfolding them.' She put the top garment carefully aside. 'One white shirt, one pair of beige trousers. Aha, wallet in the pocket.' She pulled it out and flicked it open. 'No debit or credit cards, some store cards…' She pulled a couple out and checked the inside pocket. 'A driving licence. Bingo.' She replaced the cards and put the wallet on top of the trousers, then took off her right glove and pulled out her phone. Jade could hear it ringing in the stillness.

Someone answered after two rings.

'Hello, Inspector Acaster here, at the scene of a homicide. Could well be a ritual sacrifice.' She gave Jade a significant look. 'The good news is that we have a name. Send the SOCO team, please, and get the doc down too. Two people have trespassed on the scene' – she scowled at Jade and Fi – 'but apart from that, it's fairly clean. I'll stay here. Thanks.' She shoved the phone in her pocket.

'Can we go now, please?' asked Fi. 'We've both got businesses to open, and it's likely to be busy today.'

Inspector Acaster took off her other glove and walked slowly towards them, her coat swishing as she walked. She stopped perhaps six feet away and regarded them with a look of deepest contempt. 'Not until we've had a nice little chat.'

CHAPTER 8

Once Jade had confirmed she had no plans to leave Hazeby, and that she and Fi had no intention of interfering with the investigation, Inspector Acaster let them go, with obvious reluctance, and they took the narrow path to the car park.

Fi linked arms, conscious that her friend was shivering with more than cold. But when they climbed into their respective cars, Bertha wouldn't start.

'I'll give you a lift,' said Fi, opening Jade's door. 'Why not come to the boat for a while? Have breakfast, ring a recovery garage. Maybe take the day off.'

'I have to open the shop.'

'You must be exhausted,' Fi countered. 'You've been through a horrible experience. Let Netta mind the shop and have a doze in my cabin. The river is ten times more relaxing than a CD of whale music or Rick's screeching chainsaw.'

Her attempt to lighten the mood didn't work; Jade was still huddled in her seat. 'I can't leave it all to Netta. But thanks anyway.'

They continued the journey in silence, but for the burbling radio. Jade plugged her phone into the USB socket and waited for it to come to life. Behind them, the sky brightened. Ahead, Hazeby emerged from the gloom.

'Back door, please,' said Jade. 'I need to get a grip before I can face customers, but I'll face them if it kills me.' She winced. 'You know what I mean. Thanks, Fi, you're a star. Come in and have a cup of coffee. Hugo brought a fancy little percolator thing with him. He can't stand instant.'

Fi pulled up in the alley behind Crystal Dreams and considered her answer. Zach could manage the Book Barge for a while if necessary and Dylan, for all his complaining, would chip in to help. 'You're on. I'll find the number for a recovery garage while he's making it.'

'He's probably still getting his beauty sleep,' said Jade.

However, Hugo was not only awake, but opened the door before Jade could put her key in the lock.

'Wherever have you been, Mummy? Sunrise was yonks ago.' He was dressed in a pair of burgundy trousers, a white shirt and a grey herringbone jacket with the sleeves pushed up. A checked scarf was draped artfully round his neck. 'I've been worried to death. I was about to go and find a bobby.'

Jade rolled her eyes as she followed him inside. 'It's not the fifties, Hugo. The police don't patrol every street waiting to help old ladies across the road any more. Not even here.'

'Where's Bertha? You didn't have a prang, did you?'

'She broke down,' said Jade. 'As for the police, they're a bit busy at the moment.'

Hugo frowned. 'You didn't damage an ancient monument, did you?' There was genuine concern in his face.

'No, and I didn't take any photos,' said Jade gloomily.

'Which is a shame, for more than one reason,' said Fi. 'The timestamp might have been useful to prove when you were there.'

'Why does Mummy need to prove anything?' said Hugo. 'What's happened?'

Jade hesitated, then sighed. 'You may as well know. I daresay someone will come and ask you questions.'

'Pardon?' said Hugo.

'I found a dead body.'

Hugo gave a refined squeak. 'How ghastly! Why

didn't you call me?'

Jade contemplated her son. 'What were you going to do without a car or any idea where I was? Anyway, you were supposed to be asleep.'

'I couldn't,' said Hugo. 'I felt in my bones that something was awry. Oh, Mummy! How have you managed to do this again? Come and tell me all about it. I'll make you jasmine tea and soothe your fevered brow.'

'If I'm having tea, I want builder's,' snapped Jade.

Hugo put his arm round her and turned his gaze on Fi. 'I think Mummy should have a bit of a debrief and then a rest, don't you?'

Fi took the hint. 'I do.' She gave Jade a quick hug, despite Hugo's arm, and whispered, 'Just for once, do as we tell you. I'll text you that number and call you later. Be kind to yourself.' Then she made her way back to the Book Barge, anxious and thoughtful.

***

The boat was half-full of customers by the time she arrived. Jade messaged at ten to say thanks and that she'd be in touch.

Fi expected someone to come in and share the news about the dead man, but the closest was someone buying a book on local folklore, who complained that the stone circle had been cordoned off by the police with no explanation when she wanted to commune with the elves.

Just after she'd gone, another customer said he was pleased the police were keeping drug-addled hippies away from a historic monument, and jerked his head at the door. Fi felt as if her noncommittal smile was likely to become fixed.

She closed the barge for half an hour at lunchtime, sent Zach out for a break with Stan, and bought herself and Dylan treats from Willow's Wagon. She hadn't heard from Marcus, which meant that maybe he didn't know about the murder. She wasn't going to message and tell him.

Dylan slumped over his hot chocolate and yawned. 'Now it's quiet, will you tell me why you dragged me out of bed in the middle of the night?'

Fi broke off a piece of cinnamon roll. 'Jade had a sort of emergency.'

'Couldn't Hugo have helped?'

'She needed someone with a car,' said Fi. 'The thing is, she found a body at the stone circle. She was taking sunrise photos.'

Dylan raised his eyebrows. 'She didn't put a dummy there to make it look more spooky, did she?'

Fi dropped the morsel of bun, her appetite fading as she remembered the feeling of cold, stiff flesh under her fingers. 'It was real. She just wanted someone to be with her while she waited for the police and paramedics.'

'Not another murder?'

Fi recalled the bruised, damaged face and swallowed. 'Maybe he climbed on a stone and fell on another one and…' She stopped, unable to believe it herself. It was surely unlikely, if not impossible, and why take your clothes off first? Or if you were going to take them off, why not take them all off?

'Kevin will be pleased.' Dylan snaffled the remainder of Fi's bun as she stared at it. 'He can add it to his ghost walks.'

'Have some respect, Dylan. A man is dead.' Then Fi looked at him properly and realised he wasn't eating the bun but picking it apart, his mouth downturned. *Sometimes it's easier to say something facetious than what's really bothering you.*

'It's just that… What if it's a serial killer? What if the police suspect Jade and then you? What if I have to spend Christmas with Nana and Grandma trying to organise my life, and you're not there to back me up? What if something happens to – to you too?'

'Oh, Dylan,' said Fi, touching his hand. 'Nothing will happen to me. We'll have the best Christmas, and I promise I'll keep Nana and Grandma at bay.'

The afternoon was another whirl of customers. It might be her imagination, but there seemed to be endless requests for juicy murder mysteries and at least two people in their late fifties asked for *The Children of the Stones*. Yet no one knew quite what had happened at Hazeby Stone Circle.

At four she closed, said goodbye to Zach, and with a little nervousness, watched Dylan head to town for his stint at the theatre. She was just closing the door when she saw Inspector Acaster approaching in the gloom.

'May I come in?' said the inspector, eyeing the gangplank with a nervous air that made her appear marginally more human. 'I need to ask a few questions.'

'Of course.' Fi led her into the boat and through to the galley. 'Would you like a tea or coffee?'

'No thanks. I only drink hot water and I've had enough today. Make yourself one, though.'

'I'm fine,' said Fi. 'I doubt I can add much to what I told you this morning. Jade rang me at' – she checked her phone – 'seven-twenty to say that she'd found a body, had phoned the emergency services and would appreciate some company. I arrived at—'

'I have all that,' said the inspector, opening her notebook. 'It's background detail I'm after. Did you recognise the man?'

Fi shook her head. 'No. But his face was—'

'Mmm. I gather you and Ms Fitch support each other's businesses. How long has she been selling photographs?'

'It's a new venture.'

'When did she plan this new venture?'

Fi wondered what the inspector would say if she

answered ‘a couple of days ago’, and instead said ‘I’m not sure. We’ve both been up to our ears in Christmas stuff recently.’

‘How long has she been a keen photographer?’

‘I’ve no idea,’ said Fi. ‘We’ve never discussed our hobbies.’

‘Do you think photos taken with a comparatively old mobile phone and no additional equipment would be saleable?’

Fi pondered what to say. ‘Jade didn’t get a chance to take any photos. In normal circumstances, she could have ended up with something incredible.’

‘Incredible,’ said the inspector, making a squiggle in her book. ‘Now, about her interests. You say you don’t know her hobbies, despite being a good friend, but evidently she’s interested in magic and New Age, er…’

‘I’m pretty sure she thinks most of it is hogwash, if I’m honest.’

‘Then why run Crystal Dreams?’

‘Business is business,’ said Fi. ‘I stock books on all sorts of things I’m not interested in or don’t believe in. But if there’s a market and it’s not immoral or illegal, why not? I don’t believe there’s anything mystical about those stones, but I’d buy a good picture of them. If Jade’s were any good, I’d sell them here too.’

‘But she studies the occult.’

‘I doubt that very much.’

‘So why the witchy act?’

‘There isn’t one. That’s just Jade’s choice in clothes. And selling things that people want to buy shows good business acumen.’

‘It does,’ said Inspector Acaster. ‘But if you sell what *you* consider hogwash, it might inspire someone who thinks it’s true. If they do commit murder, do you then take some of the blame?’

‘That’s like saying that a supermarket selling kitchen knives is responsible for stabbings,’ said Fi. ‘Besides, the most dangerous thing in Crystal Dreams is the amethyst geode in the window, and that’s only because it’s heavy and has spiky bits. Nothing in the shop could inspire anyone to do anything bad.’

‘I hope you’re right, Ms Booker,’ said Inspector Acaster, closing her notebook and standing up. ‘I really hope you’re right.’

CHAPTER 9

Jade leaned on the counter and watched customers wander round the shop, examining miniature cauldrons, leafing through books, holding crystal pendants to the light, and every so often, glancing at her.

She eyed the witch clock, which said that it was five to five, and wished she could make the hands move faster. Then she resolved to do the next best thing. She stood up straight and clapped her hands. 'I'll be closing in five minutes, so if you want to buy anything, please bring it to the counter.'

Everyone stopped what they were doing and stared at her. 'You never close this early,' said one of the well-groomed middle-aged women that Jade always thought of as the Three Witches. This one was rather shy, so Jade had decided she was the third witch.

'I do today,' said Jade. 'I had an early start and it's

been a busy day. The witching hour is over.'

Grumbling under their breath, a few people came to the counter with purchases. The rest put whatever they were holding on the shelves and slunk out of the shop.

'You do look tired, actually,' said the third witch.

'Thank you so much,' said Jade, ringing up her purchase: a pocket edition of *Culpeper's Complete Herbal.*

'Have you considered a tonic?'

'I haven't,' said Jade. 'Closing early will be all the tonic I need. That's eight pounds, please.'

She paid and walked away with her book, but Jade saw her glance back. 'Next, please,' she said, staring straight ahead.

By ten past five, Jade had dealt with the short queue of customers. She herded the last one out of the shop, locked the door behind her, and turned the sign to closed. 'What a day,' she muttered.

It's your own fault. Netta offered to stay later.

She opened up. It wouldn't be fair to ask her to stay late, too.

She'd have coped. Are you scared Netta might get a bit too good at her job?

No. I'm the boss.

And you've been on autopilot for most of the day. I bet you can't remember a thing you've sold.

Jade racked her brains. Apart from her most recent

customers, she had only the vaguest memory of what had passed through her hands that day. She couldn't say how long she had spent on the till. She'd had a lot of breaks, certainly, and drunk several mugs of tea in the back room on the pretext of stocktaking, while Netta dealt with things. *I'll worry about it tomorrow*, she told her inner critic. Even cashing up, which she usually regarded as a treat, seemed too much work tonight. In the end she checked all the doors were secure, then took her cash box and card reader upstairs to the flat.

Hugo, mercifully, was out. Jade splashed her face with cold water in an attempt to wake herself up, then saw her haggard face in the mirror and decided pyjamas and dressing gown were the order of the day. She made herself a large mug of milky tea, broke open the packet of chocolate digestives she had been saving for an emergency, and curled up on the sofa. She switched on the TV and settled for an episode of *A Place in the Sun* which she'd seen before. 'No surprises,' she murmured.

This week's couple had just turned down a second perfectly good house for the flimsiest of reasons when the downstairs flat door opened. *That'll be Hugo.* She sat up a little straighter, which was about as much as she could manage.

She heard footsteps, each a fraction louder than the last, followed by the grating of a key in the front door.

'Hello, Mummy,' said Hugo. 'How are you feeling?'

'Tired,' said Jade. 'Have you had a nice day?' Soon after Fi had left to return to her shop, Jade had suggested that Hugo look round the town. 'There's plenty to see. Lots of old buildings, the river is pretty, and there are shops, of course. The market might be on.'

'Oh, I love a market!' said Hugo. 'Is it organic?'

'I'm sure some of the things they sell are organic,' said Jade, mentally crossing off the stall that sold clothes pegs and plastic cutlery racks.

'I could pick up food, if you like.'

'Nothing too fancy,' Jade replied, eyeing him suspiciously. 'Nothing I haven't heard of, or that needs a qualification to open.'

'I can cook,' said Hugo. 'I've got a GCSE in food technology, remember?'

'I remember your soufflé period,' said Jade.

'The follies of youth,' said Hugo, waving a hand. 'I may return with provisions.'

Jade glanced at the paper carrier bag he was now holding. He'd found the delicatessen, then. She looked in the window sometimes when she was passing. That was intimidating enough.

Hugo raised the bag. 'Fresh pasta, Wyvernshire White eggs, pecorino, and guanciale.' Jade frowned. 'I'll make carbonara.'

She let out a sigh of relief slowly, so that he

wouldn't notice and be offended. 'Lovely.'

'And a bottle of Garganega.'

'Good lad.' Not that Jade knew what that was, but it sounded alcoholic. 'Do you need any help?'

'No, Mummy, just put your feet up.' Hugo put the carrier bag on the kitchen worktop and began unpacking it. 'It's nicer than I thought it would be.'

'The market?'

'The town. Very picturesque. Do you think you'll stay here?'

'I'd like to.' *Typical*, thought Jade. *After dragging Hugo around the country throughout his schooldays, I finally manage to settle somewhere once he's left home for good.*

On TV, the couple were looking round a beautiful villa. The husband commented that the dining room was a bit small. *At least, I hope I've settled.* Jade felt in the folds of her dressing gown for the remote control and flicked through the channels until she came to *Antiques Road Trip*. A man in a cravat was scrutinising a vase. *That'll do.*

Behind her, there were various rattles and thumps as Hugo opened cupboard doors and brought out kitchen equipment. *Please don't use every pan in the kitchen and leave it for me to wash.* 'What else did you do, apart from go to the deli?'

'Umm… Lunch by the river, a few shops, couple of churches… Wound up a bookshop guy.'

'Mr Darcy?' Jade grinned. 'What did you say to him?'

'I asked if he had a first edition of Stephen King's *Carrie* for a friend. He informed me, with his nose in the air, that he did not stock that kind of literature.'

'Oh dear.' Jade giggled, and realised it was probably the first time she had had a real laugh all day. She smiled at Hugo. 'I'm glad you're here.'

Hugo paused in rolling up his sleeves. 'It's good to see you, Mummy. We talk online, but it's not the same.'

Half an hour or so later, Hugo brought over a steaming bowl of pasta and a glass of white wine. 'Dinner is served, madam.'

'Ooh.' Jade twirled her fork and put a large tangle of spaghetti in her mouth. 'That's lovely,' she said, through the pasta.

'Thank you,' said Hugo, sitting beside her with his own bowl and glass. 'One tries.' He looked at the TV screen. 'Do we have to watch this?'

Jade handed him the remote. 'I suppose you cooked dinner.'

'All right if I put the news on? I'd like to check what the FTSE is doing.'

'Worried about your share portfolio?'

'Not worried,' said Hugo. 'I just keep abreast of these things.'

It's a different world, thought Jade, as her son

consulted his phone while twirling his fork.

They watched the weather, which promised a cold front for their part of the country, then the main presenter said, 'And now for the news where you are.'

'We could watch a film,' said Jade, as the *Wyvernshire Tonight* theme tune played.

'I love local news,' said Hugo. 'County fairs and brave dogs, and—'

'Good evening, and welcome to *Wyvernshire Tonight*,' said Martin Marsden. 'Police are asking the public to come forward after a body was discovered at Hazeby Stone Circle this morning.'

Hugo nudged Jade. 'Is that the one you saw?'

Jade didn't reply. She was too busy staring at the screen.

'The body has been identified as that of Richard Bain, a Hazeby resident who owned an IT business.'

A photograph appeared on the screen. Richard Bain, middle-aged and slight with short dark hair, raising a cocktail from his sunbed. *Poor man.*

'He doesn't look the sort of person to die in the middle of a stone circle,' said Hugo.

'The exact cause of death is uncertain, but Mr Bain was badly beaten and it is presumed that he died of his injuries. The police are treating this as a murder enquiry.'

Hugo's mouth fell open.

'We'll cross to Inspector Nina Acaster who is

leading on the case.' The screen split in two. Inspector Acaster had swapped her long coat for a black suit, but her air of general exasperation remained. 'Inspector Acaster, what can you tell us regarding the case?'

'Well, it's pretty obvious that this is a murder enquiry, as the injuries Mr Bain received were so severe. It is thought that Mr Bain died at around midnight last night. If any members of the public were near Hazeby Stone Circle after ten pm yesterday evening and saw anything which could relate to this incident, however small, we urge them to contact Wyvernshire Police immediately. This was a particularly vicious and brutal murder, and—'

'You never said anything about this, Mummy!' cried Hugo. 'You just said there was a body, not that it was an obvious murder!'

'You didn't ask.'

'I shouldn't have to!'

Jade turned back to the screen.

'The circumstances under which the body was found are . . . peculiar,' Inspector Acaster was saying. 'We are pursuing several lines of enquiry, and hope to bring this matter to a swift resolution.'

'Thank you, Inspector Acaster,' said Martin Marsden. 'The number to ring is at the bottom of the screen. Please don't hesitate to get in touch if you have any information.'

Hugo stared at the screen, then at Jade. 'Did *you* find the body?'

'Um, yeah, I did.'

'Why didn't you let me come with you?'

'It wasn't as if I knew I would find a body,' said Jade. 'I don't plan these things. They just sort of happen.'

Hugo folded his arms. 'Things have always just sort of happened to you, Mummy,' he said, and his tone was bitter.

He's right, thought Jade. 'I'm sorry,' she said.

Hugo sighed. 'It isn't your fault, Mummy. Not really.' He picked up his phone again. 'At least they don't suspect you.'

'No.' Jade twirled and twirled her fork in the last few strands of pasta. Then she realised she didn't want it and the scraping was getting on her nerves.

She put down her fork and picked up her phone. While she rarely posted on Facebook under her profile, she was active on the Crystal Dreams social media page and also lurked in a couple of local groups. She clicked on Hazeby Happenings.

The most recent post, a minute ago, was from Amy Reilly: *I can't believe there's been another murder! What's happening to this town?*

Someone called Alf Parry had replied. *Sounds like pagans to me, or Satanists.*

Here we go, thought Jade. A notification appeared

on Alf's comment: *1 reply*. She clicked to open it.

Speaking of pagans, I was walking my dog along the lane by the stone circle this morning and I saw a car drive away. I'm sure that woman who runs the witchy shop was the passenger.

Oh no. Jade looked at the commenter's name. Mandy Surtees. Not a name she knew.

There's a turn up for the books, Alf replied.

Jade swiped Facebook shut, locked her phone, and put it under a cushion. 'Let's watch something else,' she said. 'I could do with cheering up.'

CHAPTER 10

'Yes, we *are* closed tomorrow,' Fi repeated for the fourteenth time. 'We reopen on the second of January.'

'But my husband doesn't do his Christmas shopping until Christmas Eve!' wailed the customer. 'I've given him a long list to choose from and I wanted him to buy them here. Ye Olde Booke Shoppe doesn't have the right stuff at all.'

'I'm sorry,' said Fi. 'Family stuff. I'm open till seven tonight, if that helps? And if you give me the list, I'll get them ready for him.'

'Oh, right.' The woman's shoulders relaxed a little. She fiddled with one of her long dangly earrings, which had got itself caught in her scarf. 'That'll work. Is Crystal Dreams shut tomorrow too? He's bound to go there.'

'No, it'll be open. Jade has lovely gift ideas. He'll

be spoilt for choice.'

'As long as he doesn't get anything occult,' the woman grimaced. 'Given what happened at the stone circle.'

Fi tried not to narrow her eyes. 'The murder? There was no mention of the occult on the news.'

'There wouldn't be, would there?' said the woman, scrolling through her phone. 'The police wouldn't want to let the murderer know they were on to them. It's got to be some sort of ritual.'

'I'm sure it wasn't,' said Fi. 'Anyway, Crystal Dreams doesn't stock anything sinister and the crystal jewellery is very pretty. Especially the earrings.'

The woman held out her phone to show Fi a list of ten books. 'Shall I Facebook message it to the Book Barge page?'

'Yes please, and take this with my compliments.' Fi handed the woman a Christmas goody bag. It contained a bookmark and a postcard, both with a sketch of *Coralie* on the front and internet links on the back, and a Book Barge fridge magnet including a QR code. It paid to advertise. She hoped.

'Cool.' The customer tapped at her phone and smiled when Fi's lit up with the message. She turned to go. 'Oh, hello, Jodie,' she said, to a woman standing nearby.

'You're not wrong, Heather,' said the other woman. 'That murder's bound to be sacrificial. Standing stones are uncanny at the best of times, and who knows what weirdos go there at equinoxes?'

'Solstices,' said Fi, automatically.

'Same thing,' said the woman. 'Anyway, happy Christmas, Heather! See you down the Vine for New Year?'

'Happy Christmas, Jodie. Yeah, I'll be there!' Heather ran up the steps and out of the barge.

'Happy Christmas?' said a male customer clutching a book on DIY home security. 'With a murdering weirdo on the loose?'

'Go on with you, Mr Smith,' said Jodie. 'Only up at the stones. Where would you sacrifice someone in town?'

'He might belong to one of those secret societies,' muttered Mr Smith. 'The sort that don't let men like me in for no sensible reason.'

'Or he was playing one of those games,' said a second man, holding a pile of books. 'You know what I mean' – he tapped the side of his nose – 'and it went wrong. Being in a spooky setting would add to the – the frisson.'

'Outdoors at midnight in the middle of winter?' said Mr Smith. 'Gimme a break. He was lured there and sacrificed. That's what cavemen did at standing stones, isn't it?'

Zach, who had been reorganising the Christmas display to hide the gaps, looked up. 'My grandad used to camp by standing stones all over the country. He says they're quiet and peaceful.'

'He might have felt different with a murderer on the loose,' said Mr Smith. He plonked the book on the counter. 'Don't suppose you've got one on installing CCTV?'

'I'm afraid not,' said Fi. 'You're probably best going to a hardware store.'

'Any books about keeping witches out?'

'Ditto,' said Fi, with as much of a chuckle as she could muster. 'You can buy some iron. Witches don't like it.'

'You calling me a witch?' Jodie said cheerfully. 'I haven't ironed anything in ten years. If you want it ironed, iron it yourself, that's what I tell my old man.' She paused at the Christmas table as the men departed.

Zach came over. 'Should we have an occult and ancient superstition display?' he murmured. 'Meet them halfway?'

'It might add fuel to the fire,' said Fi. 'Besides, that encroaches on Jade's territory.'

Zach's face fell as if Fi had called him a fool.

'Unless I'm missing what you mean,' she added quickly. 'It's been a busy couple of days and my brain's not working. Do you mean one on myths and legends from round the world? Non-fiction, fiction and kids' stuff too? That would be a great idea! Could you do it for New Year?'

His face lit up. 'Yeah, cool! What do you want on it?'

'Your display, your call,' said Fi. 'If I don't have the books in, I'll get them. Let's educate the town.'

Zach grinned. 'Let's!'

'Did your grandfather really camp by standing stones?'

'Yup.'

'Including Hazeby Stone Circle?'

'Yup.'

'And he was never spooked?'

'Nope. But he spooked a few people who didn't expect to find someone sleeping under the stars and reading by firelight!'

Fi smiled. 'So he never felt there was something otherworldly about them?'

Zach considered. 'He told a few tall tales about what was there sometimes. He said they were friendly.'

'What? The stones?'

'Them too.'

'Wha—'

'Here you go, Fi,' Jodie put three seasonal mystery novels, a Christmas ghost-story collection, two colouring books and a handful of pretty pens on the counter, then leaned forward. 'I couldn't ask while those two twerps were in here, but what's your real opinion on the murder?'

'I don't have one,' said Fi, entering the prices. 'I just feel sorry for the man and his family. It's a terrible thing to happen at the best of times, but the week before Christmas… It makes it worse, somehow.'

'Oh yes, of course,' said Jodie, briefly abashed. 'But it's like a horror story. Witches and demons and that.'

'"Story" being the operative word,' said Fi.

Jodie sighed as she waved her card over the reader. 'You're the expert. You and Jade Fitch. What with . . . *you* know. What does she think?'

'We're not experts,' said Fi. 'But she'd agree, I'm sure.'

'I might ask her, all the same,' said Jodie. 'I don't want to think of a supernatural serial killer hanging around. If Jade agrees with you, I can put my mind at rest *and* I can buy stocking fillers. Win win. Ooh, goody bag? Thank you! Happy Christmas!'

When Jodie had left, a customer Fi had forgotten about emerged from the aft section with a collection of travel books and biographies. 'People are ghouls,' he said. 'It's like it's not real. But someone's dead. As you said, it's tragic.'

'It is,' said Fi.

'I knew him,' said the man.

'Oh no, I'm so sorry!'

'It's OK.' The man shrugged. 'I don't mean he was a friend or anything, but it's still a shock. He was a neighbour: an incomer. Moved here a couple of years ago. I always thought he must be a Londoner: you know what they're like for keeping themselves to themselves. Some round here could do with a lesson or two at that, mind. You'd think they were getting paid by the word for gossip.' The man shook his head. 'I only ever saw him when he was walking his wretched hound.'

'Wretched? What's wrong with it?' Fi's protective instincts were roused.

'It's one of those dogs that isn't kept under proper control. Woof, woof, woof for hours on end in the day, and let into the garden at midnight to do its business. Woof, woof, woof. Wakes me up and drives me doollally.' He put the books on the counter and straightened them. 'All the same, I wouldn't wish a murder on him. Oh, his poor wife. I don't really know her either, but she's a bit chattier when I see her out and about. And now she's all alone without even any kids to comfort her. Poor thing. Anyway, I was glad you shut Jodie up. She doesn't mean badly, but like I said, people are ghouls. Mind, if people are going round murdering people from my street, maybe I should get CCTV. If you get any books in about it, I might come and get one after.'

He left and the shop fell silent. Fi let out a deep

sigh.

'I'll put the kettle on,' said Zach.

'Thanks.' Fi picked up her phone to check the list Heather had sent and saw another message in her personal inbox, from Marcus.

Just heard from Dave (Sgt Blake) and looked at news. Sorry I'm not there. Gather NA is taking the lead. Watch out.

What did that mean? Watch out because of Inspector Acaster? Or a murderer? Or the temptation of getting involved in an investigation? Probably the latter. He was warning her off as if she were an enthusiastic idiot. Was that how he'd described her to his colleagues? She scowled.

There was a familiar clatter on the stairs. Dylan descended at speed and, seeing no customers, burst into the chorus of 'The Power of Love' by Frankie Goes to Hollywood.

'An old 'un but a good 'un!' said Zach, emerging from the galley with two cups of coffee.

'Our band's going to do retro covers!' said Dylan. 'Not that Mum thinks the eighties is retro.'

'I was only little when that came out,' said Fi. 'But it's the sixties that are retro, in my view. Er, Dylan, what are your friends saying about the murder at the stones?'

Dylan wiggled his fingers in front of his face. 'Supernatural beings doing weird rituals. But never mind, Mum…' He burst into the first lines of the song and Zach joined in.

'Oh, for pity's sake,' said Fi. 'I'm taking the dog for a walk. Dylan, you can help Zach with the shop. Back in ten. Don't forget to give out the goody bags.'

She stomped into the kitchen, clipped on Stan's lead and hurried onto the towpath, avoiding anyone who seemed to be heading for the Book Barge.

A walk along the river would clear her head. She slowed down as she let Stan off the lead, and pondered. *Surely the murder wasn't in any way ritualistic*, she thought. *But look where the body was found. How can I blame people for what they believe about the original purpose of standing stones? I don't know much myself. What if someone did act out an ancient ritual?*

She checked her watch. It was around the time when she and Jade usually took a short break over a virtual cuppa. She might as well tell Jade what Richard Bain's neighbour had said, and warn her that people might seek her 'expert' opinion too.

The phone rang and rang, eventually going to voicemail. Presumably the shop was too busy for Jade to answer. They'd have to catch up later.

'Hi, Jade,' she said into the phone. 'Hope you're OK – I expect you're rushed off your feet. Watch out for people with silly questions: I've had a few. Ring me when you can. We're spending the day with Mum and Dad tomorrow, but we'll be back before you close. See you soon, bye.'

She felt uneasy. *Nothing makes you feel quite so stupid as talking to an answerphone*, she thought. *That's all it is. That, and people's stupid theories.*

Fi shook herself and went to haul Stan out of a bush. She'd chat with Jade over a glass of wine later and then they'd both feel better. Wouldn't they?

CHAPTER 11

They came, mostly, in pairs.

'I can see another one outside,' murmured Netta. 'Nose to the window.'

'I wish they'd just come in,' said Jade. 'It's the peering that gets on my nerves. That, and the sidling up to the counter. Oh yes, and the whispering.' She glared at a pair of young women who were sneaking glances at her between turning the card rack.

When she had opened at half past nine, taking her own sweet time, the shop had been quiet. *Maybe they think I won't open today. Hopefully everyone's done their Christmas shopping.* She rebuked herself for such a non-commercial thought, but it was the truth.

However, by ten o'clock two brave souls had ventured through the door, whispered to each other in the far corner, and finally approached the counter with a pack of incense sticks, the cheapest thing in the shop. 'Can we have this, please,' said the boldest, a woman wearing a black parka over a velour tracksuit, but she still flushed.

'Certainly,' said Jade. 'That'll be £1.99. Cash or card?'

The woman looked blank, as if she had forgotten that transactions in a shop involved money. 'Oh, um, card. Yes, card.' Her accomplice nudged her. 'I just wondered…'

Here it comes, thought Jade. She folded her arms. 'Yes?'

'Is it true, what's on Facebook?'

Jade's first impulse was to say *You might have to narrow it down for me*. But as she opened her mouth, she realised she really didn't want the woman to do that. 'I wouldn't believe everything you read on Facebook,' she said, and pushed the card reader forward.

'Oh.' The woman paid and gave her a small smile. 'So you weren't—'

'Would you like a bag?'

'Oh no, thanks, that's fine.'

'Excellent. Have a good day.'

The pair walked slowly to the door, murmuring to each other as they went. The woman who had bought the incense sticks glanced at Jade, then quickened her step.

Jade sighed. 'Is this what today will be like?'

'Possibly,' said Netta. 'Shall I make us both a drink?'

'I'll go,' said Jade. 'If someone asks for me and they don't have a police badge, tell them I'm busy, will you?'

'Will do.' Netta faced an imaginary customer and adopted an expression which would have made a casual browser quake.

Jade escaped to the back room, filled the kettle, and got two mugs from the cupboard.

She had filled Netta in, to a degree. First, she hadn't murdered anyone. That was the most important bit. Second, yes, she had been at the stone circle on the morning when the body was discovered. And yes, she had found a body and called the police.

Netta looked as if Jade had told her that she regularly roamed the skies on a broomstick. 'Oh my days,' she said, gawping at Jade. 'You – you—'

'Yes, I did,' said Jade, 'and I'll probably never hear the end of it. However, I don't want to talk about it. I just hope the police find out who did it and arrest them. Then things can get back to normal.'

'How . . . how exciting,' breathed Netta.

'How troublesome, you mean. You weren't the one being grilled by the police before the sun was even up.' As she said those words, the pit of her stomach seemed to shift, though she couldn't have said why. 'If anyone asks, refer them to me. Please don't repeat what I've told you.'

'Oh no, of course I won't.'

'That includes social media, obviously. And I'd rather you didn't fish around on there for people's daft theories. It's the police's job to sort this out, not Fred and June from number 42, or whoever's putting in their two penn'orth.'

Netta looked puzzled. 'What's a two pen-off?'

'Another way to say two pence.'

'But why would they put 2p into… What *would* they put money into?'

'Never mind. Just smile and say nowt. I mean nothing.'

The two young women were still at the card rack, actually watching her through it. Jade considered removing the cheapest items from the shop floor. If buying an item was the price of coming to the counter for information, she might as well make a decent profit.

'Netta, will you do me a favour?' she murmured.

'Sure, what is it?'

'This probably sounds strange, but I'd like you to take all the small packs of incense sticks and cones to the stockroom.'

'But we've—'

'I know it's odd, but I have a reason. When you've done that, I may ask you to remove a few more things.' Jade opened the counter drawer and took out the black notebook with silver stars that she used to keep track of everything in the shop. In the back was a list of current stock with prices. Jade took a pencil and ran it down the list, ticking everything that cost under three pounds. As she scanned and ticked, she mused on the funny feeling she had had earlier. What had she been thinking of? No, it had been when she was talking to Netta. Something about the police—

Bile rose in Jade's throat, stinging. She swallowed, but her mouth was dry. 'Just getting a drink of water,' she gasped, and hurried to the back room.

She leaned over the sink, but apart from a half-hearted retch nothing happened. She ran the tap and held a glass underneath, then managed a few gulps of water.

When Inspector Acaster turned up at the stone circle yesterday, I felt like a person of interest. And yet she's done nothing. She hasn't come to take a statement, or... Thoughts of what Inspector Acaster could do crowded into Jade's mind. *Or anything*, she told herself firmly.

The door opened and Netta stuck her head in. 'Are you all right?' she said quietly, exaggerating every movement of her mouth.

'I'm fine,' said Jade. 'Back in a moment.' She finished her glass of water and refilled it.

The day rolled on. In spite of Jade's counter-offensive with the cheaper merchandise, she sold a lot more cards and packs of tealights than usual. A couple of people asked straight out, 'Is it true you saw the body?' and Jade replied, with perfect honesty, that she'd rather not talk about it. But despite her stony exterior, the thought of what Inspector Acaster might be doing gnawed at her until she wanted to scratch herself all over.

It was almost a relief when a police car pulled up outside. Of course, Netta had gone out for lunch.

'Look!' cried a customer, and pointed so dramatically that they resembled a gun dog, tense and quivering.

All the customers crowded to the window. They were too excited to keep their voices low.

'I knew it!'

'Maybe she's here for a crystal-ball reading.'

'Crystal balls do the future, dummy, not the past.'

'Do you think she—'

The door opened and Inspector Acaster walked into the shop alone. Jade's heart sank. She had hoped that if the inspector did visit, she would be diluted by a sergeant or a constable. Hopefully, one who knew Jade and would make allowances.

Inspector Acaster reached the middle of the shop and gazed around her, smirking. 'Interesting establishment,' she said. 'Any chance of a chat?'

Jade clasped her hands behind her back so that any trembling would be invisible. 'Yes, of course.' She looked past the inspector to her gaping customers. 'I'll close for a while.'

An *Ohh* rose from them. *Like a bunch of disappointed kids*, thought Jade. 'When will you reopen?' said one.

Jade shrugged. 'How long will you need?' she asked the inspector.

Inspector Acaster inspected the nails of her left hand. 'Hard to say. Not more than half an hour. Possibly not that long.' Some customers' faces expressed disappointment that Jade wouldn't be cross-examined for longer.

'Right, you heard the officer.' Jade made shooing motions. 'Go and buy gift tags or something. Off you trot.' If she could have swept them out with a broom, she would have.

When the last customer had trailed out, Jade put the latch on and turned the sign round. 'Shall we go in the back?'

'I'm fine here,' said Inspector Acaster.

'Cup of tea? Coffee?'

'Not long had a drink, thanks.' Jade suspected the inspector would have been just as breezy if she had been arresting her for murder. That made her shudder, and she hoped Inspector Acaster hadn't noticed.

'It is a bit cold, isn't it?' The inspector pulled out her notebook and came right to the counter. 'Mind if I lean on here?' She was in heels today, which brought her practically eye to eye with Jade.

Why did this have to happen when Marcus is on holiday? Jade remembered what Inspector Acaster had called him. She had never thought of him as a pussycat, but next to this woman—

'Your shop's busy.' Inspector Acaster glanced at the window, where someone was peeping in. They hurried off at once.

'It's the run-up to Christmas,' said Jade. 'I'd be worried if it wasn't.'

'Is it busier since the body was found?'

'I don't think there's a correlation.' Jade felt sweat trickle down her back. She hoped it wasn't a hot flush. The inspector would probably take sweating as a sign of guilt.

'So…' The inspector wandered about the shop, picking things up and putting them down. She lingered at the book section. 'What sort of people are your customers?'

'Usually female,' Jade replied. 'We get teenagers, quite a few young women, some older ones. Mostly, they're dabblers.'

'Any . . . hardcore ones?'

Jade folded her arms. 'I don't know what you mean.'

A mirthless laugh. 'I'm sure you do.' She returned to the counter. 'Full-on pagans, Wiccans, Satanists, druids. That sort of thing.'

‘Like I said, dabblers. This is a small market town of mostly well-to-do people.’

‘With standing stones nearby. You can’t tell me there aren’t any cults or sects around here.’

‘If there are, they’re keeping it quiet.’

‘Hmm.’ The inspector scribbled a note, ending with a question mark. ‘Are you a practising witch, Ms Fitch?’

‘No, I’m not. Before you ask, I never have been. What I am is a shopkeeper. I’ve had sweet shops, gift shops. Trading is what I do.’

The inspector wrote another note. Her writing, unlike Inspector Falconer’s, was impossible to read upside down. Jade suspected that was deliberate. ‘I take it you won’t mind if I delve into your history.’ She paused to let that sink in. ‘How long have you lived in Hazeby-on-Wyvern?’

‘Since the summer.’

‘That isn’t long.’ Inspector Acaster put down her pen and leaned on her elbows. ‘I spent time this morning looking at a couple of cases. The murders of Freddy Stott and Jon Angel. Had you been in town long when Freddy Stott was murdered?’

Jade willed herself to keep her eyes on the inspector, though all she wanted to do was find an escape route. ‘About a week. Perhaps a little longer.’

‘That’s a coincidence.’ The inspector didn’t bother writing anything this time. *She already knew*, thought

Jade. *She's trying to rattle me. And she's succeeding.*

'How's the case going, Inspector?' she asked, to buy herself time.

Inspector Acaster considered. 'We're waiting for the results of the post-mortem,' she said. 'Lots of staff already off for the Christmas break. For now, we're assuming the cause of death was a combination of hypothermia and blood loss, probably combined with shock.' She seemed to ponder what to say next. 'I'm sure you're aware that the victim was a local man. Richard Bain, an IT guy. Did you know him?'

'No, not at all.'

'Sure?'

'As far as I can be. I mean, I might have passed him in the street, or been in the same pub at the same time, but I've never met anyone with that name.'

'What about his wife? Madeline Bain, Maddie for short. Medium height, short curly red hair, early forties. Could be one of your dabblers. Here.' Inspector Acaster pressed a few buttons on her phone and a photo appeared. 'That's them together.'

'Doesn't ring a bell,' said Jade. 'If she's ever come in, she certainly isn't a regular. I've got a good memory for faces.'

'I imagine you have, in your line of work.' She gave Jade a speculative look, and another bead of sweat snaked down Jade's back. 'You're a cool customer, Ms Fitch.'

‘I wouldn’t say that.’ Jade had the strong impression that she was being backed into a corner. ‘I’m surprised you haven’t asked me to give a formal statement yet. As the person who found the body, I’d have thought that would be a priority.’

‘Would you.’ Inspector Acaster continued to gaze at Jade. ‘I have my own priorities,’ she said, at last. ‘My top priority, of course, is bringing Richard Bain’s murderer to justice. Before they kill again, preferably. I will do everything in my power to make sure that doesn’t happen. Everything.’ She snapped her notebook shut. ‘Good day to you, Ms Fitch. You can carry on selling your charms and cauldrons now.’ She walked to the door and opened it. ‘Shop’s open!’ she yelled, and went on her way.

Jade ran to the door. People were already bustling forward. ‘No it isn’t,’ she shouted. ‘I’m on my lunch break.’ She slammed the door and secured it. Then she rushed to the back room and burst into shivering sobs.

CHAPTER 12

Early on Christmas Eve, Fi and Dylan drove away from town. It was only a few miles to Spetisham-on-Wyvern, a slightly larger town downriver where she had arranged to meet her parents and have lunch. Zach would look after Stan at home until Boxing Day. He would take Stan to visit his grandfather, Stan's former owner, in the nursing home, and Annie wouldn't be stressed about having a dog in the house on Christmas Day.

Fi still hadn't heard from Jade, despite another call and a message. Jade was probably upset, exhausted from the shop, and busy catching up with Hugo, but it was unlike her not to just say so. Fi hoped Jade wasn't so traumatised by her experiences that she was hiding, though she was hurt that Jade might not feel she could tell her. On the other hand, perhaps it was more natural that she poured her heart out to Hugo instead.

'Listen, Mum…' said Dylan.

She glanced at him. He'd taken his earphones out. She braced herself for questions about what she'd seen at the stones.

'You know I said I didn't want to lose you the other day…'

'Please don't worry. I'm sure it's a one-off murder.'

'Maybe, but the thing is… I'm not the only kid without a dad in school, but that's 'cos their parents are divorced or separated. My dad's dead. I mean, you're a pain, but I'd sort of rather you stayed alive.'

'I intend to.'

The roads were busy with people rushing to be somewhere else for Christmas, as Marcus had done. Fi often found car journeys the best place for a neutral conversation with Dylan. *Come on*, she told herself. *Get it over with.* 'Do you want me to tell you about your dad? I don't mind.'

Dylan shifted in his seat. 'Yeah you do.'

'Honestly,' said Fi. 'Tell me what you know and I can go from there.'

'He left when I was a baby, and he was with someone else when he died. So I guess he left us for her, which makes him a—'

'Anything else?'

'Nana seems to think he's half a halo short of being an angel. How can someone who dumped his wife and kid be Mr Perfect?'

'He's her son,' said Fi. 'You'd be surprised how perfect mothers think their sons are.'

'You don't think I'm perfect. You call me all sorts.'

'Only to your face. I'm ever so nice about you to other people.'

'Yeah, right.' Dylan heaved a sigh. 'So what *was* he like?'

Fi saw that his fists were clenched in his lap. She wished she could give him a hug, but maybe he didn't want one. 'He was a bit of a joker, clever, really sociable. He was funny, whereas I'm serious and boring.'

'You aren't boring,' said Dylan. 'Apart from being a parent. You started a book barge when you were quite old.'

'Forty.'

'OK, *very* old. You're not totally rubbish at video games. One of your best friends is a sorta witch. I mean, the list goes on. You're almost fun.'

'I'll take that as a compliment.'

'So anyway, Dad. I guess he didn't want a baby.'

'He was thrilled, Dylan, honestly. It's just the age-old story. He met somebody he liked better than me and left.'

'Nana can't have approved.'

'She was terribly upset,' said Fi. 'I think after a while she tried to pretend it hadn't happened and that if he'd lived, he would have come back to us.'

‘But there’s no way of knowing, because they went off to Italy and drove into a river. And they only ever found her body, ’cos his is out at sea.’

‘Yes,’ said Fi. ‘Whenever I’m exasperated with Nana’s fussing, I remind myself how I’d feel if anything happened to you. She loved your dad, no matter what. And I love *you,* no matter what. Unless you become an axe murderer, perhaps.’

‘Or murder someone on a standing stone.’

‘Yeah, that too.’

‘Whatever. Stop being soppy, Mum, or I’ll be sick.’ Dylan put his headphones in and turned to the window. Fi hoped he’d ask again when he wanted to know more. Not that there was much more to tell. But it upset her that he thought he was to blame for the marriage breaking down. Gavin had been running away from more than just a baby.

Spetisham was bustling. A Christmas Eve market on the quay was heaving with people, and it took some time to find her parents.

She felt a little guilty for dragging Dylan along: he’d prefer spending time with his friends to pottering with his mother and grandparents. However, he seemed happy enough, the earlier conversation submerged.

She watched couples mooching about the stalls and felt desperate pity for Mrs Bain, now a widow, surrounded no doubt by Christmas decorations as the dog barked for a master who'd never come home.

But for a while she forgot Dylan's questions and the murder and enjoyed her parents' company. In the market square, a Ceroc band was playing. Fi stood arm in arm with her father, laughing as her mother taught Dylan how to dance. He took it in good part. Admittedly, it wasn't likely that any of his friends were there to see him. If they were, they might think it a laugh to join in.

'Any news on that murder?' said her father, jolting her back to reality.

'Nothing more than I read on the internet first thing. I hope they find the killer soon. You wouldn't believe the stupid things people make up. After a while it's catching, and I worry over Dylan walking to the theatre and back.'

'Did you know Annie's on Facebook?'

'Sort of. Why?'

'She's following the Hazeby Facebook page.'

'Does it matter?'

'Have you seen what they're saying about the murder? People think Jade was driven away from the scene first thing that morning. I'm worried for her. She's too nice for that sort of gossip.'

A chill went through Fi. It wasn't just worrying for Jade, but for her too if her car had been recognised. The police might reveal who had discovered the body, and that would make things worse. She certainly wouldn't tell anyone until she had no choice; especially if people would add two and two together and make five. She managed to say 'People never cease to disappoint me.' She sensed her father's sidelong glance, but he said nothing.

They had lunch at an Indian restaurant to contrast with the full Christmas roast the following day, and because Fi's parents had nothing similar where they lived. Afterwards, Dylan left them to buy presents and visit a record store, while Fi and her parents went to an art exhibition.

But the time of happy oblivion had passed. Local newspapers were everywhere, the murder splashed across their front pages, and wherever they went someone was discussing it. Fi steered her parents' discussion to Dylan's band and their business, but in her head the previous morning kept replaying itself: the shadowy stones, the cold figure on the rock, Jade's stricken face.

Fi and Dylan returned to the boat at four, and she was glad that she had set the timer on the coloured lights to welcome them home. After Dylan had left for the theatre, she sat on the deck with a cup of coffee, thinking how pretty and innocent the town looked. Was it too early to go to Jade's? She scrolled through her phone. There was still no message.

Was Richard Bain sacrificed? Surely that only happens in books nowadays, except once in a blue moon, under unusual and terrible circumstances.

Feeling furtive, she opened an incognito browser and made a quick search for historical ritual murders. Northern European bog bodies were the main result, murdered and put in peat bogs for reasons lost to antiquity. But that was thousands of years ago. Then there were the victims of sacrifice in South America, who were killed in a different way again. No matter how long ago it had been, Fi felt even more disappointed with people and closed the search.

Surely a sacrifice should be quick and clean so that the victim is pure for the gods, she thought. *Poor Richard Bain looked as if he'd been beaten up. And the underpants and the pile of clothes beside him make no sense. A sacrifice would be fully naked or clothed in something ceremonial, wouldn't it?*

She stared at the town, but her mind was back at the scene.

He could have been murdered elsewhere and his body dumped at the stones, but why? Lugging a body over that stile wouldn't be easy, and why take the clothes and risk leaving your DNA on them? Why not use this massive river? Were the stones convenient, a coincidence, or misdirection?

She searched for the latest local news.

Mrs Bain was pictured in one article, a little pixelated, which suggested the photograph had been taken with a long lens. She was standing at a window, appearing to dab her eyes.

Mrs Bain had gone to bed when her husband took the dog for a late-night walk, said the article. *She assumed he had gone to his local pub, The Star and Fishes, where he sometimes went for a quiet pint. When she woke, however, he was missing. She thought he had gone to the spare room to sleep rather than disturb her, but he wasn't there either. Then the police arrived with their terrible news. Mrs Bain is reported to be devastated. The couple would have celebrated their silver wedding anniversary at the end of January.*

She had to speak to Jade. She hurried into town and along the buzzing high street. The shops, restaurants and pubs were lit up and the pavements were thronged with people. Carol singers chorused outside one of the little churches.

Maybe Crystal Dreams would be at peak busyness, with panicked last-minute shoppers, but Fi could help if necessary. Afterwards, she and Jade would go out for a drink. If that meant facing the gossips, better to get it over with.

But when she arrived at Crystal Dreams the lights were out, and a scribbled sign on the door said *Closed until further notice.*

CHAPTER 13

Jade was trying to make sense of her rental agreement when her mobile rang. She fished it out from under the pillow, hit *Refuse* without checking who was calling, and replaced it. Then she stared at the document.

The minimum term of the lease is six months from the date of occupancy. When had she moved in? Was it June? July? Whichever it was, she didn't have long left. She picked up a pen and wrote *Check when I got the keys* in the black notebook with silver stars. *This might be the last list I make in here. And I still had pages to go.*

She turned back to the document. *After this date, either party must give at least thirty (30) days' notice—*

The doorbell rang.

'Leave it, Hugo,' she called.

'What if it's important?'

'Yeah, right. The only people who'd bother me are people I don't want to see.'

The doorbell rang again, several times.

The bedroom door opened and Hugo appeared. 'Seriously, Mummy, are you going to hide for ever? If you're planning to hibernate, you should have started earlier than this.'

'Very funny.' Jade imagined herself as a big brown bear hunkering in her room, eating everything she could find in preparation for a long winter. It didn't sound too bad.

Hugo left, then came back and stood in the doorway. 'It isn't the police,' he said. 'At least, there isn't a police car outside.'

Jade's blood ran cold. Somehow she'd managed not to think of that possibility. 'Don't let them in!'

'You'll have to come out and stop me,' said Hugo. She heard the flat door open, followed by descending footsteps.

In the absence of a better tactic, Jade slid down and put the covers over her head. Why, oh why did Hugo have to be here? Why hadn't she settled for Christmas greetings on FaceTime and a voucher by email? *Serves you right for boasting about your growing business and your new flat*, she thought. *Pride comes before a fall.*

Footsteps grew louder. There were two sets, one

lighter. 'Maybe you can talk sense into her,' Hugo said to whoever it was.

That isn't the police. Jade relaxed a little. Until that point, she hadn't realised that she was rigid with fear.

Someone, not Hugo, tapped at the door. 'Jade, will you let me in? It's Fi.'

Jade removed the duvet from her head. 'I don't want to talk to anyone. There's no point,' she said, and replaced the bedclothes.

'She's been like this since yesterday,' said Hugo. 'I came back from a sightseeing trip and found the shop shut and Mummy in her room. She's only come out to go to the bathroom and make tea and toast.'

Fi knocked again. 'Jade, I promise I won't try to make you come out, but I have to talk to you. It's about the murder.'

'That's the last thing I want to discuss,' said Jade. 'I've seen what people are saying on social media, and Inspector Acaster is busy digging into my past to pin this on me. You know what? I need a break from it all. A permanent break. So I'm leaving.'

There was silence. *Good,* thought Jade. The last thing she needed was Fi trying to talk her round, because she would miss her so very much. Out of the blue, she felt a lump in her throat. *Oh, for heaven's sake, woman.*

'That's why I have to speak to you,' said Fi. 'This murder . . . it doesn't add up. Something's wrong about it.'

'Well, yes, it's a murder. Not good. Especially for me, right now.'

'That isn't what I mean. I was reading the newspaper, and… It's fishy.'

Jade frowned. 'In what way?'

'I'll tell you if you let me in.'

Jade considered this under the duvet. 'OK,' she said at last. 'But no tricks. And you have to go when I say so.' She pulled the cover down enough to see the door.

'I'll make tea and leave you to it,' said Hugo, outside.

'Thanks,' said Fi. She entered the room and stood at the foot of the bed.

Jade heaved herself into a sitting position. 'Sorry I'm not dressed to receive visitors,' she said, glancing at her faded flannel pyjamas.

'That's OK. Do you mind if I sit down? I've been out with the family all day.'

'Sure.' Jade drew up her knees and Fi sat carefully in the space. 'So what is it?' She heard the grumpiness in her voice. *She's only trying to help*, she told herself. 'What was in the paper?' she asked, more softly.

'It's not so much that, though it was interesting. Don't roll your eyes at me, I haven't finished.'

'Sorry, Mum.' Jade sighed. 'Go on.'

'The murder looks like a sacrifice of some kind, right? Body stripped and stretched out on a stone altar?'

'With you so far.'

'But if so, why did they leave the guy's underpants on? I mean, it's not as if they were worried about offending anyone. And they made a right mess of him.' Fi explained her reasoning.

'I bet your search history is a sight to behold.'

'I used an incognito browser. Anyway, half the village will have questionable internet search activity this week.'

'So you don't think it's a sacrifice?' Jade pondered. 'Now you've said that… But Inspector Acaster does. Or at least, that's what she told me when she came to the shop yesterday. Unless that was a trick to lull me into a false sense of security. Which is very possible.'

'What else did she say?'

'She asked if I was a practising witch, and said she was going to delve into my history.'

Fi put a hand on Jade's arm. 'I know that was upsetting, Jade, and I wish it hadn't happened, or that someone had been there to stand up for you when it did. But did the inspector say anything about who might have done it?'

Jade thought. 'She asked about my customers, and wanted to know if any proper druids, witches or Satanists ever came to the shop. I told her no.'

'Oh good,' said Fi. 'If one of your customers did this, I'll eat my hat.'

'Don't do that. Give it to me instead. Especially if it's the nice one with the big bobble.'

Fi held out a hand. 'Done.' Jade leaned forward to shake it and realised that she was sort of smiling.

'I come bearing tea,' Hugo called through the door. 'Shall I leave it outside?'

'You may as well bring it in,' said Jade.

Hugo entered, bearing a tray on which were two of what Jade thought of as her best mugs, another mug with milk in, and a plate of chocolate digestives. He put it on the bedside table. 'If you need anything else, let me know.'

'Thank you, Hugo,' said Fi.

'My pleasure.' He executed a little bow and left the room.

'You've got him well trained,' said Fi. 'Biscuits don't last five minutes at home, not with Dylan.' She added milk to her mug and stirred. 'Want me to do yours?'

'No, it's OK.' Jade made her brew, took a biscuit, and settled against her pillow.

'Inspector Acaster's barking up the wrong tree,' said Fi, and reached for a biscuit herself. 'Actually, I don't think she suspects you at all.'

'In that case, she's about the only person in Hazeby who doesn't,' retorted Jade. Then she paused.

'Why do you think that? She as good as told me she's after me. She hasn't arrested me, but she turned up at the shop yesterday and started insinuating.'

'Concentrate on "she hasn't arrested me".' Fi dunked her biscuit for a second and bit into it with a satisfying crunch. 'You found the body. Why does that annoy her so much?'

Jade mulled it over. 'I'm still not following. Since I've been in here, my brain's morphed into a pillow.'

'It's possible,' said Fi. 'I'm not sure she thinks you're guilty. I reckon she's having a go at you to stop you poking your nose in.'

'Oh!' Jade stared at Fi. 'Really?'

'I wouldn't be surprised. She's playing hardball.' Fi's brow furrowed for a moment. 'I've heard actors say that on TV a hundred times. I never thought I'd get to say it myself.'

'What has she said to you, if anything?'

'She popped in the other day and asked about you. Specifically, your photography idea. But now I think she did that because she knew I'd tell you. I reckon she wants to get you properly scared. Too scared to investigate and feeling you're in her sights, so you tell her anything you know rather than keep it to yourself and investigate. You're probably the person best placed to solve this, and Inspector Acaster doesn't want that.' Fi's mouth turned down. 'I wish Marcus was here. When he comes back, I'll tell him never to go on holiday again. Not unless he takes me too.'

'Stop planning your summer break.'

'Just thinking ahead.' Fi reached for the rental agreement. Jade thought about moving it away, but that would take energy she didn't have. 'Is this what I think it is?'

'Might be.'

'So you're really moving on?'

'Yup. I'm going as far from this place as I can get. I'll open a sweet shop or a gift shop. I've done those before. I'm never touching a cauldron or a crystal again as long as I live.'

Fi gave her a very steady look. 'If you run away, you do realise Inspector Acaster's won?'

Jade shrugged. 'She's won already. I've never felt so low. I mean, there were bad times, times when I've packed the car, fetched Hugo from school and run out on things, but this... This is different. I think she actually believes I'd do something like that.'

Fi moved up the bed and hugged Jade. For a slender person, she gave good hugs. Slowly, Jade returned the hug, and somehow found that she was crying.

'It's all right,' murmured Fi. 'Let it out. You'll probably feel better afterwards.'

'I'm not upset,' Jade choked out. 'I'm furious! What sort of person even does this? I should report that woman to – to someone.'

‘Then do it,’ said Fi. ‘Think of that poor man’s wife, alone at Christmas, while Inspector Acaster plays God.’

‘Right.’ Jade released Fi and got out of bed. ‘That does it. I’m going nowhere. We’ll crack this case before she does. Justice my – my *foot*. Inspector Acaster’s out for what she can get, and if she gets the glory of this case, it’ll be over my dead body.’

‘Steady on,’ said Fi, looking taken aback.

‘She’s already had a head start. We’ll give her two more days, Christmas and Boxing Day, and then she’d better watch out. Now, if you don’t mind taking yourself to the lounge, I’m getting dressed. I don’t know about you, but I need a stiff drink.’

CHAPTER 19

Christmas Day and Boxing Day passed in a blur of too much food, plenty of wine, and silly board games that had even Annie laughing till tears ran down her cheeks.

It was a welcome respite from worry. Dylan asked no more questions. Both parents and in-laws kept off the subject of the murder. Fi wore the beautiful amethyst earrings that Jade had given her and was relieved that Jade's messages over the two days seemed relaxed, happy and even facetious, when Hugo attempted a complicated festive feast from a glossy supplement using the equipment available in the flat.

Fi and Dylan returned to *Coralie* at sunset on Boxing Day and collected Stan from Zach. It was good to be home.

She woke on the twenty-seventh of December

feeling like a child when the summer holidays come to an end and a new term in a new class beckons. It was that mixed sensation of coming out of carefree laziness, yet looking forward to the challenge of something new to tax her mind.

A little part of her felt guilty that they were investigating when they'd told Inspector Acaster they wouldn't, and Marcus's cheerful Christmas messages had hinted that he hoped she was keeping her distance this time. But as she prepared to take Stan on a mid-morning walk, Fi knew it was time to start thinking about the murder again.

Was Mrs Bain still in town? Wouldn't she have gone to family or friends for Christmas? Surely it would be too difficult to stay in the house?

'Rrrerrfff,' woofed Stan, shivering against her legs as they stood on the deck.

'Good point,' said Fi. 'What about the dog? I assumed it came home, but no one's said so. If it did, perhaps she couldn't go away at Christmas. Look at Annie – she didn't really want you at hers. Naughty Annie.' She crouched and scratched between Stan's ears as her thoughts darkened.

The dog might have been a sort of witness to the crime. It couldn't talk, but it would surely react to anyone doing its master harm. According to the customer who was their neighbour, it was a barker. If it saw someone hurt its owner, wouldn't it try to protect him? What would the murderer do to keep it quiet?

But I'm sure the papers would have said if anything had happened to the dog. Maybe it went home before anything happened. Perhaps it runs off sometimes. Or maybe it's fonder of Mrs Bain anyway. I could go past the house to see. But how could I tell if the dog was out of sight?

Stan gave a throaty growl then a tiny yap, and wagged his tail. Fi looked up. One of the dogs they often met on walks was approaching. He was some distance away, but Stan had caught his scent.

Fi knew the lane where the Bains lived. It was at the southern edge of the town, starting with the Star and Fishes and opening onto countryside at the other end. It was part of a route Fi took when she wanted a more challenging run in the hills. There would be nothing more natural than for her to take a post-Christmas walk that way. If she passed the Bain house and the dog was inside, even if she didn't hear it bark, Stan might smell its presence. It was a possibility, anyway.

'Time for you to join the detective team,' she told Stan. 'I'll message Jade and she can join us… Oh no, that won't work. She's reopening Crystal Dreams today.' She leaned in through the wheelhouse. 'Fancy a walk, Dylan?'

'No,' Dylan called back. 'I'm cycling to Alfie's.'

Even better, thought Fi. *Alfie's house isn't far from that lane, and I want to discuss the band with his mum. It's a bit of a detour, but hey.*

'Come on. You've been stuck indoors playing video games for the best part of two days, and you've devoured half a turkey and four million roast potatoes. I'm taking Stan for a walk not far from Alfie's and I need to talk to his mum anyway. And I've got to pass the bakery…'

'So you might accidentally buy cakes? Go on then.'

'Great. We can chat on the way.'

Dylan pulled a face. 'It's been wall-to-wall adults talking for two days. I've got to learn the lyrics for the band and get with my mates for some decent conversation. Are you sure we can't practise on the boat?'

'Perfectly sure,' said Fi. 'That's what I need to discuss with Alfie's mum. Her house has space and she won't get slapped with a noise abatement order like I would, but she might not want a bunch of sweaty teenagers going New Romantic at high volume. I'll promise her that when you're good enough to perform in public, I'll get a licence for you to do it on the deck. I'll even help with lugging equipment if necessary.'

'Meh,' grumbled Dylan, shoving his earphones in as he joined her on the deck.

When Fi emerged from the bakery, Kevin the ghost-tour guide was standing by his blackboard, drumming up trade.

'Come back at three,' he urged a small group of people. 'I've got ghoulish tales galore, new and old. What about the grey lady who haunts the site of a witch's cottage at Christmas? Or the old man in white robes who's seen in the old station at solstice, with a mysterious scythe? The old station's built on a ley line, you know. Or how about the woman weeping outside the graveyard wall? I've got 'em all.'

'Is the grey lady a witch and the man in white a druid?' asked one of the bystanders.

'Could be,' said Kevin.

'Are you including the stone circle in your tours?' said another. 'Tell us what witches and druids did there in the olden days.'

'Might do, might do,' said Kevin, then spotted Fi. 'Maybe not just now, though: the police are all over it like a rash. It's a bit of a hike out there, anyway. I've got plenty of tales right here in town to make your hair curl. Plus special seasonal offers on my normal rates. An absolute bargain, madam…'

Fi rolled her eyes, prodded Dylan, who was leaning against the wall with Stan, and continued walking.

The lane boasted a higgledy-piggledy collection of individual cottages, well spaced out and between two and four hundred years old. All had been gentrified and some were worth a small fortune. A few were holiday lets, currently empty and cold-looking. Fi scanned them, trying to spot the window she'd seen in the pixelated photo of Madeline Bain. Dylan, singing under his breath and munching on a millionaire's shortbread, seemed oblivious to their detour from the normal route to Alfie's.

As it turned out, Stan's detection skills weren't needed. They were only four cottages down the lane before it became clear that the Bains' dog was safe and well. A volley of barking boomed from an early Victorian villa whose door was opening.

Stan stopped and leaned against Fi's legs, as he often did when nervous.

A poodle bounded into the lane to the full extent of his lead, stopped barking to sniff the air, then saw Stan and started barking again, his tail wagging hard enough to fall off.

Stan uttered an inquisitive 'Rrrerrfff?', his own tail tapping Fi's leg, and made to move forward.

The poodle rushed towards them, towing a woman. She stumbled on the step, swore, yanked the lead and pulled the door shut. She was dressed in a knee-length patterned corduroy skirt, a fluffy green jumper, low-heeled boots and a puffer coat. Her short curly red hair was restrained by a navy earwarmer headband. Fi had a feeling she'd been a customer once or twice, but couldn't be sure. Perhaps she'd simply seen her round town.

Mrs Bain followed her dog's gaze and her scowl turned into a frown.

'Hi,' said Fi.

'Hi.' The woman appraised them. 'You seem familiar. You're not a reporter pretending to be someone else, are you?'

'No,' said Fi. 'Oh! Are you—? I'm so sorry for your loss, Mrs Bain. It was a terrible thing to happen.' She *was* sorry. She hoped that sounded more authentic than her feigned surprise.

'Thanks.' Mrs Bain remained tight-lipped. 'Are you walking your dog in the hills?'

'No,' said Fi. 'Just up the lane, then round the corner to town.'

Mrs Bain looked relieved. She probably didn't want company. She was nicely made-up, making Fi feel scruffy and ungroomed. The poodle tried to reach Stan and let out another volley of barks. 'Pack it in, Basil,' she said, yanking the dog back.

'What a lovely dog,' said Fi. 'I imagine he must be grieving too.'

'He's a blessed nuisance,' said Mrs Bain. 'I never wanted a dog in the first place, but Richard thought it would be good company. I blame lockdown.' Her scowl deepened. 'Why he had to get one that barked so much, I've no idea. I can't chuck him out in the garden to do his business or the neighbours complain.

So here I am walking him day and night.'

She contemplated Dylan, who was rummaging in the bakery bag, oblivious to his surroundings. 'Does your lad want a job? No, forget it: I'll manage till I work out what to do. Just flipping typical Richard. Think up a million stupid ideas, get bored, then leave someone else to sort out the mess. I don't suppose you know what I mean.' Without waiting for an answer, she pulled Basil away and marched briskly up the lane.

I do know what you mean, thought Fi. *Gavin left all sorts of mess behind when he died.* She gazed at the Bains' home. It was pretty, and at the side was a large parking space: a positive luxury in the older part of town. In it were two expensive-looking cars. *Gavin didn't leave me with anything like those to help settle his debts. I had to wait seven years until he was officially declared dead. And yes, I was angry, but I grieved for him, despite everything. You're just angry.* She chided herself for selfishness. Perhaps Mrs Bain wasn't at the stage of expressing her grief, but her annoyance was irritating.

'What's *her* beef?' said Dylan, pulling his earphones out.

'That was Mrs Bain,' said Fi. 'The one whose husband was murdered.'

'Oh,' said Dylan. 'So she's angry with the murderer?'

‘I’m not sure,’ said Fi. ‘She seemed more angry with the victim.’

CHAPTER 15

'Mummy, you're fidgeting.'

'Am I?' Jade folded her arms.

Hugo resumed typing and she narrowed her eyes. 'Are you working?'

'Not really,' he said, his focus on the laptop screen. 'Just checking in.'

'Don't tech companies do Christmas?'

'Christmas isn't a thing everywhere in the world.' He laughed. 'You're tapping your foot now.'

'I can tap my foot if I want in my own flat.'

'I'm not saying you can't. But you need something to keep you occupied.'

'Such as…?' Behind her casual words, Jade's brain was busy. What she wanted, more than anything, was to get to the bottom of the murder at the stones, but she had a distinct feeling that Hugo wouldn't approve. Besides, she didn't like the idea of venturing out alone to investigate. When she had gone for a drink with Fi and Hugo on Christmas Eve, she had seen the sidelong glances and heard the whispers in the Swan. And what if Inspector Acaster had put a watch on the flat? What if she was waiting to catch her? She shivered.

'You could open the shop,' said Hugo.

'I could… But Netta's on leave until Monday. And I'm still not sure what I'm doing about it.'

'Crystal Dreams?' Hugo's eyebrows shot up his forehead. 'Isn't it doing well?'

'It was. Now, with all this…'

'Have you considered that if you don't reopen, people may think the rumours are true? And your regular customers will start going elsewhere.'

'There isn't an elsewhere. This is the only crystal and magic shop for miles around. People travel here specially.' She heaved a sigh. 'And I enjoyed it. But if it's over…'

'Worst-case scenario: you have to close. Doesn't it make sense to sell all the stock you can? Then you'll have money for a new venture.'

'No one likes a smart alec,' said Jade, and he grinned. 'I do see the sense in what you're saying, but – but I don't want to be in the shop on my own.'

Hugo shuffled up the sofa and gave her a squeeze. 'You won't have to. I'll come too. If anyone starts anything, I'll deal with them.'

Jade looked at Hugo's slim frame and wondered how he would manage that. Then she remembered that he had carried a heavy suitcase upstairs without effort and smiled at him. 'Do you really think it's the right thing to do?'

'Yes,' said Hugo. He typed for a few more seconds, then pressed various combinations of keys and closed his laptop. 'Swap those pyjamas for one of your outfits, Mummy. Time to get to work.'

An hour and a half later, Jade had served precisely two customers. 'I suppose it's the lull between Christmas and New Year,' she said. That felt like an excuse. *What if people aren't coming in because of...* She stood up and paced to drive that thought away. And as she walked, she realised that while she hadn't gone overboard with snowmen, reindeer, or Santas, the shop definitely had a Christmassy vibe. 'I should probably switch focus to "New year, new you".'

'There,' said Hugo. 'I knew you'd have a brilliant idea.'

'You can choke on too much positivity,' said Jade. 'Make yourself useful and help with the boxes. I've got stock to put out.' Before he could get up, she ruffled his hair.

Jade was gazing at her spread of self-help books on the counter, trying to decide what to put in the window, when the door opened. She felt herself tense but it was only Jimbo and Dawn, the hippyish couple who lived in an old caravan on the waste ground next to where she parked Bertha. If anything, they appeared to be taking refuge.

'Hello there,' she said. 'What can I do for you? Please ignore the mess, we're changing the shop displays.'

'It's cool, man,' said Jimbo, the plait in his beard waggling as he spoke. 'You gotta do what you gotta do.'

'Yes, indeed,' said Hugo.

Jimbo raised his eyebrows, then turned to Jade. 'We're not here to buy, like. Money's a bit tight.'

'Yeah,' said Dawn.

Jade looked them both up and down. They were pale, and the assortment of layers both wore hung off them. They'd been thin to begin with. 'That's fine,' she said. 'I just wondered if I could help you with anything. And if you want to stay in the shop, where it's warm—'

''T'aint that,' said Jimbo. 'We can stay warm in the library till five. We wanted to say thank you.'

Jade frowned. 'What for?'

'For not setting the cops on us. Woman in a suit came knocking on the van door Christmas Eve. Threatened to kick the door in. When we let her in, not that we had much choice, she fired questions at us. Are you Druids, are there many of you, where do you meet, what do you do when you meet?' Jimbo started wheezing. Jade was about to offer him a glass of water when she realised he was laughing. ‘I told her that if she was after Druids 101 she could go on the web.’

‘She didn’t appreciate that,’ said Dawn. ‘That’s when she pulled out a search warrant.’

‘Oh no,’ said Jade. ‘I’m really sorry.’ She paused. ‘Sorry to ask, but… Was this about that murder?’

‘Presume so,’ said Jimbo. ‘She was very keen to know where we were on solstice eve. Luckily, we’d hitch-hiked to see my mum down in Brighton and she put photos on that Facebook. Man, the copper looked like she’d swallowed a wasp.’

‘So you don’t celebrate the solstice at the circle?’ Jade asked.

‘Nah,’ said Dawn. ‘Too ruddy cold. I ain’t freezing to death.’ Her eyes widened and she put a hand to her mouth. ‘I didn’t mean that. The silly cow kept saying she knew we lived an alternative lifestyle ’cos we got arrested in that tree protest a couple of years ago. Jimbo told her that means we respect nature, not that we go round bumping people off for kicks.’ She snorted. ‘I don’t believe there’s anyone round here who would.’

‘I couldn’t agree with you more,’ said Jade. ‘I was about to make a brew. Would you like a tea or a coffee? And we’ve got mince pies for our special customers.’

Jimbo waved a hand. 'You're all right. Don't do caffeine and we're vegan.'

'I'm sure we've got some tins of veg that need using,' said Hugo. 'I can go and check.'

Jimbo scratched his head. 'I don't wanna—'

'That would be grand,' said Dawn.

'I might be a few minutes,' said Hugo.

Jimbo and Dawn each accepted a mug of hot water and sipped carefully until Hugo returned with a bulging carrier bag. 'Here you go,' he said, handing it over. 'Tomatoes, chickpeas, beans, peas, new potatoes.'

'You're a gent,' said Jimbo. 'Won't forget this.' He sighed. 'That inspector said popular opinion reckoned that poor guy was a sacrifice. Honestly, people. Anyway, better let you get on. Thanks again, Jade. And you, young man.'

'It's a pleasure,' said Hugo. 'It was lovely to meet you.'

'You went to the shops, didn't you,' said Jade, once the pair had shuffled out. 'I don't buy tins of new potatoes.'

Hugo held up his hands. 'Busted. Excellent detection, Mummy.'

'Why, thank you.'

Jade sipped her mug of tea, contemplating the array of books before her. From what Jimbo and Dawn had said, the likelihood of Richard Bain's murder being a sacrifice was incredibly slim. So what was behind it? 'A man,' she said, aloud. 'Badly beaten, but only around the head and face.'

Hugo made a face. 'Oh Mummy, do you have to?'

'Sorry. Sometimes it helps when I think out loud.'

Hugo heaved a theatrical sigh, fished in his pocket, and put in a set of earbuds. Jade gave him a thumbs up. 'Let's go again. A man with severe injuries, but just to the head. Stripped almost naked and clothes left in a neat pile beside the body. Wallet left there too, with store cards and a driving licence. What are we supposed to think?'

She banged her mug so hard on the counter that tea slopped over the side. Quickly, she pushed the books out of range. 'I'm a complete fool.'

Hugo took out an earbud. 'Are you all right, Mummy?'

'We're supposed to think that body is Richard Bain.'

Hugo frowned. 'It must be. Surely someone identified it.'

'Yes, his wife. Fi told me.' Jade mopped up the spilt tea with her sleeve and took a meditative sip. 'Unless…' She set the mug down again, this time more carefully. 'Three options. One: the body *is* Richard Bain, who met a horrible, strange and illogical end. Two: his wife was so distressed that she identified the body of another man as her husband.

And option three… Come on, Watson.'

'She's lying?'

'Precisely.' Jade beamed at him.

'I'm not sure I want to be Watson,' said Hugo. 'I'm not cut out to be a sidekick.'

'Don't you worry.' Jade picked up her phone and began typing rapidly with her thumbs. 'I already have a partner.' A few seconds later, her phone pinged. 'The game is afoot.'

'I beg your pardon?'

'Don't worry about the window display, but put these books on the shelves at eye level, facing out. Anything on empowerment or achieving goals, stick it in the middle. You can take the gift wrap to the stockroom.'

Hugo goggled at her. 'This wasn't quite what I—'

'You'll have a wonderful time. You used to love playing shops when you were little.' Jade took a ring of keys from her pocket and slapped it on the counter. 'The little one's for the cash box, the ones with purple tops are for the shop. Everything's priced and you can Google how the card reader works.'

Hugo sighed. 'How long do you propose to be out?'

'No idea,' said Jade. 'Expect me when you see me, and text if you need anything. Fi and I have got a murder to solve.'

CHAPTER 16

'It's me! Coming, ready or not!' Jade descended into the boat so fast there was a risk she'd land flat on her face before finishing her sentence.

Fi set down a pile of books gratefully and gave her a hug. 'Is this about my message? Who's running the shop?'

'Hugo,' said Jade. She was bouncing. 'He's more practical than he looks. And yeah, I want to know what you meant by that cryptic stuff you texted me, but I also want to tell you…' She peered round the shop. 'What are you doing? I thought I was the one threatening to pack up and leave.'

'I was re-jigging the shop while I waited for you,' said Fi. 'It can wait. Let's talk outside. Less risk of Dylan coming home and hearing us. Have you had lunch?'

'No.'

'Nor me. We'll grab something from Willow's Wagon and eat while we talk.' She grabbed her coat and bag. 'Walk, Stan?'

Stan put his paws over his head, closed his eyes and feigned sleep.

'Come on, you lazy lump.'

Stan rumbled a resigned 'Rrrerrfff,' stood up, stretched and wagged his tail.

Fi attached his lead, messaged Dylan, then joined Jade on the riverbank. They walked along the towpath discussing what they'd discovered.

'So Madeline Bain isn't exactly grief-stricken and the police are likely to only have her word for his identification,' said Jade. 'Seems fishy to me.'

'She doesn't *seem* grief-stricken,' said Fi. 'Some people can't express emotional stuff, so they show anger and don't know where to direct it. The murderer, obviously, but sometimes the victim too, for getting themselves murdered and leaving the bereaved person alone.'

'You're just being nice.'

'Emotions are complicated. *People* are complicated.'

'Mine aren't,' said Jade. 'And I'm not.'

'I was angry with Gavin for dying and leaving me in a mess,' said Fi. 'But I was sad too. We'd loved each other once. We made Dylan. A teeny tiny bit of me had wanted him back. Everything tangled until I didn't know how I felt.'

'Not everyone is as weird as you,' Jade replied. 'The Bains were together for twenty-five years. You'd expect devastation, not anger.'

Fi stopped walking and stared into the rushing river. 'I felt sorry for her. I never had to identify Gavin because his body was never found.' She shuddered. 'If your suspicions are right, presumably Madeline convinced the police by identifying more than Richard's face, as it was so badly injured. Maybe she said she recognised a scar or a mole or something. Surely the police will double-check, though, using DNA?'

Jade frowned. 'DNA results take ages, don't they? I get the impression Inspector Acaster wants to close the case quickly and seize the glory before Marcus comes home and takes over.'

'Pam.'

'Her first name's Nina. They said on *Wyvernshire Tonight*.'

'I messaged Marcus to ask exactly who or what I should watch out for. He said PAM, told me it stands for Passive-Aggressive Menace, and added that he was sure I knew who he meant.'

Jade snorted. 'Come on then, show me that cottage. "Really expensive cars" could mean anything.'

'What do *you* know? Bertha's battery flattens

quicker than pancake batter.'

'I may have a Bertha income,' said Jade, with dignity, 'but that doesn't mean I don't have Lamborghini tastes.'

'What if Madeline sees us and wonders why I'm back?'

'Say you're after her neighbour because you've ordered him a book on – what was it he wanted?'

'CCTV installation.'

'There you go.'

'But I haven't. What if I bump into *him*?'

'Make it true. Order it while we're walking.'

Looking down the lane from the Star and Fishes, it appeared busier than earlier. The period between Christmas and New Year was a time for visiting, but there was a better than average likelihood that some of the people ambling about were journalists.

Walking Stan for a second time that day in a place she rarely visited wouldn't do as a reason to be there. Fi considered suggesting to Jade that they could pretend they were going for a run in the hills. However, having contemplated Jade's pink and lime-green ankle-length dress and Doc Martens, she decided the customer excuse, while unlikely, was more believable. She searched online for a book on CCTV and bought it.

On the other hand, she heard no barking, so hopefully Madeline was out with the dog. They'd have to risk it. Fi looked up the lane and saw a post box a little way past the Bains' cottage. 'That'll do: we can pretend to post a letter.'

They strolled up the lane, Jade fumbling in her bag. She lifted it as if to peer in and glanced over the top of it at the Bains' parking space. 'Nice cars,' she commented.

'I'm sure they are, but keep walking.' They reached the post box and Jade stood by it, still searching. 'It's OK, no one's looking. Do you know what the cars are?' Jade nodded. 'Let's go, then.'

'So were they expensive?' Fi murmured, as they walked away.

'Oh yes,' said Jade, not breaking stride. 'A BMW 4 Series Gran Coupe and a Ferrari California.'

'If you say so.' Fi barely recognised the badges.

'Yup. At least a hundred grand there, probably nearer two, but I bet they haven't got the character of Bertha. Or even your car. What's she called again?'

'My car,' said Fi. 'Let's pop into the pub and see what we can find out there. I'm thirsty and Stan will help. He's our undercover agent.'

'Good idea,' said Jade. 'A soft drink, though: I'll be in the shop later.'

'Me too,' said Fi, 'or goodness knows what order my books will end up in.'

The Star and Fishes was truly traditional rather than styled that way. A log fire crackled under a stone mantlepiece and the low beams overhead were blackened by age. On the walls were old photographs of riverboat men and cricket teams from previous generations. There was a dartboard in the main bar, a sign to a skittle alley, and in a dark corner, a snooker table. The only other woman in the place was the bartender, and a fair number of the drinkers looked as if they intended to be there till closing, but would make a pint of bitter last several hours.

While Jade went to the bar, Fi sat down at a sticky table near the fire and nodded to an old man sitting in a high-backed settle nearby. A brindled whippet on a piece of string rose to his paws and came to greet Stan.

'What's your dog's name?' asked Fi.

'Clover,' said the old man. 'Yours?'

'Stan.'

'Aaah. He's well-behaved. Terriers mostly yap. He *is* a terrier, isn't he?' He emptied the dregs of his beer and peered at Stan with rheumy eyes.

'Sort of,' said Fi. 'But he's not yappy.'

'Ah.' The old man sat back as another elderly man joined him with two more pints, and Jade returned with a Diet Coke and an elderflower cordial.

The men viewed their soft drinks with as much disapproval as a teetotaller would have shown towards their beer. 'Place is going downhill,' said the second man, possibly more loudly than he realised. 'Next they'll be serving frappalappacino and chicken tinker on a wooden board and it'll be full of women and worse. Kids.'

The first man chuckled. 'Sorry about Ned, ladies,' he said. 'Anyway, glad he's not a yapper.'

'Who, me?' boomed Ned.

'No, you old fool. The dog. Yappy dogs are worse'n kids.'

'I heard there's a noisy local dog who comes in with his owner every evening,' said Fi. 'That must drive you nuts.'

'The Bains' poodle?' said the old man, taking a tiny sip of beer and wiping the froth from his mouth. 'No idea where that story came from. Saw it in the paper meself. T'ain't true.'

'What she say?' bellowed Ned.

'That bloke what got himself murdered,' enunciated his friend. 'Someone said he come in here regular with that poodle of his.'

'He never,' said Ned, sounding affronted. 'He used to walk it past every evening, regular as clockwork, but he never come in.'

'Maybe he went to a different pub,' suggested Jade, sipping her Diet Coke.

The two men shook their heads. 'We ring the changes, me and Ned,' said the first old man. 'And I never saw him elsewhere. Perhaps he drank at home with his wife.' He pulled a face, as if accusing the

Bains of something improper. 'My missus likes me out from under her feet, thank the heavens.' He raised his beer.

Fi grinned and raised her drink in response.

She and Jade chatted about nothing in particular for a while, finished their drinks, then made their way outside and walked down to the quiet riverbank.

'Why would Madeline say he went to the pub every evening when he didn't?' said Fi.

'Maybe that's what he told her he was doing and she believed him.'

'Now *you're* being nice,' said Fi. 'It's one more fishy thing. Jade, I know what you've been through, but… Should we revisit the crime scene?'

Jade looked very serious, but after a moment she nodded. 'OK. That's if it's not tied up in police tape and Inspector Acaster's not there, waiting to do sacrifices of her own.'

'Apart from her, if any police officers are there we can talk to them,' said Fi. 'Let's go while it's still light. I'm sure we won't be on our own: I bet it's swarming with ghouls. I mean, people with a macabre mindset, not actual—'

'Calm down,' said Jade, 'I get it. What about Stan?'

'I'll leave him on the boat when I get the car keys,' said Fi. 'He's probably worn out.'

They rushed back to *Coralie*, settled Stan, then

hurried to the car park. The day had become increasingly overcast, and it would be dark before they knew it.

In silence, they drove out of town. *That first trip to the stones feels as if it happened a hundred years ago*, thought Fi. *Like a dream, or rather a nightmare*.

The road seemed even more twisty and narrow than before. In daylight she could see the deep ditches on either side, their edges crumbling in places. The journey took longer than she remembered.

As she approached a bend, Fi realised in horror that a pickup truck had cut the corner and was coming towards them at speed on their side of the road.

Fi steered as far left as she dared and braked. Nothing happened. She braked again. Nothing.

Seconds slowed to hours. She saw the panic in the other driver's face and heard Jade gasp. The engine screamed as she put the car in first gear to make it slow down. Then she did the only thing she could and steered into the ditch.

The left-side tyres slipped into the gully and the left wing hit the bank. Fi was flung forward, then back.

The truck whizzed past with millimetres to spare and disappeared round the bend.

After another million years, she looked in the wing mirror. Someone was running towards them. She tasted blood in her mouth where she'd bit her lip. An acrid smell filled the air.

Jade was speaking and the radio burbled inanities, but Fi couldn't make out any words. All she could hear was the thud of her heart and blood rushing in her ears.

CHAPTER 17

Slowly, Jade opened her eyes. She had been so prepared for impact that she had taken the car's lurch forward and down to be merely the first stage. She glanced across at Fi. Apart from a tiny smear of blood on her lip, she seemed unharmed.

We appear not to be dead. That was what she wanted to say, but when she spoke, she got as far as 'W-w-we.' She took a deep breath and tried again. 'Not d-dead,' she managed.

'No,' said Fi. 'Are you OK?'

Jade wiggled her toes and flexed her fingers. 'Think so. Nothing hurts, anyway. You?'

'Yeah, nothing broken.' She fell silent. 'We were lucky. Not sure about the car.' She undid her seatbelt. 'We should get out, just in case.'

'If you can.' Jade looked out of the window. The car had tipped forward, but she had no idea how deep the ditch was. 'Have you seen *The Italian Job*?'

Fi opened her door. 'Ah.'

A man in a check shirt, jeans, and a bodywarmer arrived at Fi's side of the car, panting. 'I saw you go into the ditch. What happened? Did you hit a skid?'

'I was taking evasive action, since you were cutting the corner,' said Fi. 'My brakes cut out.'

'I didn't cut the corner,' he said, and put his hands on his hips. 'I'm a very safe driver. This road's in a terrible state with the rain we've had. Anyway, you're both all right, which is the main thing. Want a hand out?'

Fi peered at the road ahead then turned, wincing, and looked out of the back window. *Hoping for speed cameras or CCTV*, thought Jade. *She'll be lucky.*

'Yes,' Fi said, eventually. 'Please.'

The man opened the driver's-side door, braced himself, and extended a hand to Fi. She took it, and he yanked her out of the car without ceremony. 'There you go,' he said. He eyed Jade. 'You'll have to get yourself over to this side.'

Jade manoeuvred herself over the gearstick, trying to keep her skirt at a respectable level. The car groaned occasionally as she did so, and she found herself holding her breath.

'Give us your hand. Right, on the count of three…'

The car tipped a little as Jade put her weight on her right foot, but the man heaved hard and she reached the roadside safely. 'Flipping heck,' he said, miming wiping the sweat from his brow. 'I'm glad I don't rescue damsels in distress every day of the week.'

'Maybe you should take an advanced driving course, then,' snapped Fi.

'There's no need for that,' he said. 'Not when I've been a good Samaritan. I didn't have to come back.'

'Leaving the scene of an accident?' Fi's voice rose. 'Driving without due care and attention?'

His eyes narrowed. 'I know you. You're one of them—' His gaze moved to Jade. 'And you're the other one. Those two busybodies who stick their noses where no one wants them.'

'I suppose you'd rather people got away with murder,' said Fi. 'Then again… Care to give me your name, car registration and insurance details?'

'Your word against mine,' said the man. 'I've lived in this town all my life. Know these roads like the back of my hand. And no one else was around to see.' He leaned forward. 'If you'll take my advice, *love*, go to the hospital and get yourself checked out. I reckon you've got a bit of concussion.' He tapped his head then walked off, glancing over his shoulder every so often, as if to be sure they weren't following him.

As soon as he had disappeared, Fi stamped her foot. 'That – that – aargh!'

'I know. And yes, he is.' Jade pulled her phone from her pocket and opened the notes app. 'Black pickup truck, small dent in the bonnet… I don't suppose you got the reg? I had my eyes closed.'

'It ended in JF,' said Fi. She sighed. 'It's hopeless.'

'It isn't,' said Jade. 'He said he lives in Hazeby. I bet we could track him down.' She added *Thinning sandy hair, stubble, lumberjack shirt, jeans, brown work boots, brown bodywarmer* to her note. 'I reckon he was on his way to a job.'

'I think you're right. There was white writing on the back of the truck.' Fi watched Jade type. 'Can I use your phone to ring the garage? Mine's in the car.'

'Course you can.' Jade pressed a couple of buttons and handed it over. 'The number's in my recent calls log.'

'Oh yes…' Fi dialled and held the phone to her ear. 'How's Bertha?'

'Poorly.'

Fi opened her mouth to reply, then switched to listening mode. 'Hello… Yes, I wondered if you could come and recover my car. The brakes failed and it's halfway in a ditch… Yes, on the Monkton road, not far from the turning for Hazeby Stone Circle. It's a blue Fiesta… Yes, I have a passenger, also female… OK, thanks. See you soon.' She ended the call and handed back the phone. 'He says he'll be with us in twenty minutes or so.'

'That's pretty good,' said Jade.

Fi went to the boot and took out a reflective

triangle. 'Better put this out. I don't want another driver to come round the corner and hit us. Just in case it *is* a problem with the road.'

Jade walked with her, wrapping her arms around herself to keep warm. 'I don't think it's anything to do with the road.'

'So it was the other driver's fault?'

'Partly, yes. Not entirely.'

Once they were round the bend, Fi walked a little further and set down the triangle. They began to walk back. 'I'm guessing your car's pretty reliable,' said Jade.

'She is. She sailed through her last MOT. No problem starting, no problem braking. Until now.'

Jade thought this over. 'I don't know much about cars, mechanically speaking… Is it possible to mess with the brakes without going under the bonnet?'

'I have no idea,' said Fi. 'It doesn't seem likely.'

They walked in silence for a while.

'I could understand if it was my car,' said Jade. 'Being as I'm the town's resident witch and social pariah.' She imagined Inspector Acaster creeping up on Bertha in the dead of night, with a pair of wire cutters and a wicked glint in her eye. 'But you're an upstanding member of society. As far as anyone but Inspector Acaster is aware, you've had nothing to do with this.'

Fi managed a laugh, but it wasn't a convincing one.

'She's not a fan of us, Jade, but I really don't think she'd cut my brakes. Or yours.'

They arrived at the car. 'We should probably stand clear of it,' said Fi. 'Someone might have planted a petrol bomb for good measure.'

Jade shot her a look. 'I hope you're joking.'

Fi shrugged. 'I'm not sure any more.'

They took up position about twenty metres beyond the car. 'I'm guessing you've gone off the idea of visiting the stones,' said Jade.

'All I want to do right now, to be honest, is get the car to the garage, go home, and spend the rest of the day under a blanket,' said Fi.

'That doesn't sound such a bad idea.' Jade saw herself reclining in bed while Hugo brought her meals on a tray. Then again, she'd wallowed in bed lately, brooding, and hadn't enjoyed it one bit.

She studied Fi, who was standing on the verge, grim-faced and arms folded. 'Will you text Dylan?'

'No point,' said Fi. 'He'll only worry, and I can tell him when I get home. Hugo?'

'Same.'

The flatbed truck from the garage came into view a few minutes later. 'Wow,' said Jade. 'They're never early. And given how temperamental Bertha is, I would know.'

'You'd probably save money if you bought a more reliable car,' said Fi.

'Maybe,' said Jade. 'Or I could cut costs by not having a car at all. Everything here is within easy reach.'

Fi raised her eyebrows. 'So you're staying?'

'I didn't say that. But yeah, for now.' And for the first time since the accident, Fi smiled.

Slowly, slowly, the truck pulled in and backed up. 'Hello, George,' said Fi, as the driver jumped down and came towards them. He was a dark-haired, stocky man in his mid-thirties, wearing green overalls.

'Hi there, Fi,' said George. 'Well, this is a sticky situation. What happened?'

Fi grimaced. 'Swerved to avoid an idiot in a pickup truck and my brakes failed.'

'Your brakes failed?' George stared at her, then at the car. 'But I replaced your discs and pads when I serviced her last month.'

'So you did,' said Fi, frowning.

Jade longed to say *I told you so*, or mutter darkly about foul play, but decided it was probably best not to do so in front of George. 'Will you be able to tell us what did it?' she asked.

'Should be, yeah, but not straight away. We're already fully booked for today.' He glanced at Jade. 'Not to mention that we haven't looked at yours yet, and I'm the only one in. Mum and Dad have gone away for a bit of winter sun, and everyone else has booked time off with the kids.'

'I understand, George,' said Fi. 'Thanks for coming out so quickly in the circumstances.'

'No problem. Couldn't leave you two out in the sticks, could I? Especially at the moment, what with – you know. You two sit up front and I'll get the car on. I daresay you wouldn't mind a lift to Hazeby.'

'Yes, please,' said Fi.

They climbed into the truck and squeezed together on the front seat. 'Will you report this to the police?' Jade asked, as she watched George attach two hooks to Fi's car.

'The dangerous driving, yes,' said Fi. 'Nothing else until I'm absolutely sure that someone's tampered with the car.'

And that probably won't be for ages, thought Jade. She imagined them rattling back to the village, further and further away from whatever evidence might be waiting at the stone circle. *Someone definitely wants us out of the picture. But who?* She eyed Fi, who was looking straight ahead, stony-faced. *And should we listen to them?*

CHAPTER 18

Dylan came back from Alfie's at seven. He wasn't needed at the theatre that evening, and despite coming home with a bag of chips, waved the Chinese takeaway menu in a meaningful way as Fi tried to concentrate on a video call with her parents, who had finally arrived in Normandy.

'That was very rude,' she told him, after saying goodbye. 'You could have waited till I'd finished the call. They've been travelling for twelve hours. They probably wish they had a takeaway nearby.'

'*Zut alors!*' said Dylan, unabashed. '*C'est la belle France!* They'll be in a restaurant scoffing pork in cider and cream before we've finished choosing what to eat.'

'I'm not hungry,' said Fi. 'Choose what you fancy and I'll pick at it. Er, is that the takeaway that does delivery?'

Dylan turned the menu over. 'Yeah. Why? If you prefer the other one, I can fetch it on my bike.'

'No, it'll get cold,' said Fi, hoping she sounded nonchalant. 'The delivery guy brings it in one of those thermal things. Much better.'

Dylan shrugged and continued his perusal. Fi rolled her head and shoulders, trying to ease the whiplash. It was mild, but even so. She checked her phone to see if the garage had called while she was speaking to her parents. They hadn't.

'Oh yeah,' said Dylan, as he jotted down his choices, 'where's the car?'

'Car?' said Fi, feeling the blood drain from her face. 'What car?'

'Are you all right, Mum?' Dylan looked up from his scribbling. '*Our* car. The chippy's next to the car park, remember. It's not in its usual place.'

'You aren't usually that observant in daylight. How could you tell when it's pitch black?'

'Callum Thomas and the Hazeby Massive were zooming round on e-scooters and Callum went into the back of a dark car. I went to check it wasn't ours.'

'E-scooters aren't allowed on public roads in Wyvernshire.'

'Callum's a twonk who doesn't know what county he lives in, but he's built like a tank so I'm not telling him. So where *is* the car?'

'Garage,' said Fi, wondering whether to pretend it

was in for another service. But if she lied to Dylan, she couldn't complain if he lied to her. 'A different twonk was on the wrong side of the road earlier and I ended up in a ditch on the Monkton road.'

Dylan's mouth dropped open. 'Are you OK?'

'Bit achy, but I'll be fine. And so will the car, I'm sure. I wasn't going fast enough to do any serious damage.' *I hope.*

'Wish you'd had a dashcam.'

'Tell me about it; I've got two on order as we speak. Talking of orders, give me yours and I'll ring the takeaway.'

'Sure you're OK?' Dylan hugged her gently then ruffled her hair. 'Bet it was Callum's brother or cousin or something. All the Thomases are twonks.'

'I'm fine. The police will sort it out, I'm sure.'

'Won't they be too busy with the murder?'

Fi pulled a face, hoping that would cover her anxiety. 'I think traffic is different. I'll have to ask Marcus— I mean Inspector Falconer.'

Dylan handed over the order paper. 'I wrote down extra-crispy chilli chicken for you. You'll be hungry once you smell it. And I'll let you choose a movie and watch it with you, no matter what drivel you pick. You need cheering up, especially if you're on first-name terms with the fuzz. Then we can play a video game. But maybe not a racing game.'

'Maybe not.'

Much later, after she and Dylan had watched two films and he'd gone to bed, Fi went out with a torch. *Coralie* was moored tight to the bank, with several heavy ropes taut around metal bollards. Anyone planning to change that would require an axe, lots of energy and plenty of time. All the same… She told herself to relax, locked up again and went to her cabin.

A message from Jade appeared: *You OK? I'm aching.*

Me too. Nothing from garage. See you tomorrow.

Marcus messaged with a photograph of a man far out at sea on a surfboard. *This is what I did today. Nearly drowned. Hope you're keeping safe.*

Fi frowned, wondering if he'd heard about the accident somehow. *Doing my best,* she typed. *Are traffic cops different from CID?*

We share constables cos of cutbacks. Why? Been caught speeding?

Just curious. Goodnight.

You too. See you soon.

Fi settled down with her book, but the words might as well have been hieroglyphics. She couldn't follow the story and didn't care what was happening to the characters. Perhaps it would be better to go to sleep. She turned out the light and lay listening to the river sloshing past, tensing at every other sound she heard.

Count and breathe, she thought. *Make your mind*

switch off.

After a while, she drifted into a confused dream. A yapping poodle drove the car into a bottomless ditch and they fell through the air and— She woke with a jerk. She'd been asleep for a total of ten minutes.

Heaving a sigh, Fi got up. Staying in bed would be torture. Besides, what had woken her? Had something bumped *Coralie*? Or was someone outside? She put on her dressing gown, switched on the lights in the main part of the boat, took the torch and went on deck. There was no one there.

Hazeby was now invisible but for one or two windows. The Christmas and street lights were all off. The other boats along the bank were in darkness too. The only light was the beam of her torch and the glow from the windows. She picked her way around the deck and shone it into the river. Bits of broken branches floated by, some nudging the hull. Fi felt the rush of air from an owl's wings as it swooped overhead, then heard a hoot.

Shivering, she went below.

With a soft, inquisitive woof, Stan left his basket and came over. She picked him up, the warmth of his little body comforting her.

'I'm so glad I didn't have you in the car,' she said, kissing his head. 'Even with your harness, you'd have been hurt. Come on, help me find something to read that'll calm my mind.'

Carrying him, she wandered round the boat, seeking a book to help her sleep.

The mindfulness section seemed apt, but the calm, unruffled women on the covers, eyes closed, content to their cores, were less aspirational than irritating. 'Bet you wouldn't look like that if you'd ended up in a ditch and someone might have tampered with your brakes,' Fi wanted to tell them.

Perhaps poetry… No. Everything she picked up was either insipid, emotional or disturbing.

Maybe non-fiction. Too bad the book on installing CCTV hadn't arrived yet. It might teach her something, or send her to sleep. How to solve a murder in three easy steps without riling the police would be more useful. Or how to find out if someone's lying… No, that was probably in psychology.

Fi paused at the hobby section. She probably ought to have a hobby beyond running or cycling but she never seemed to have time, and calmer, more stationary hobbies like painting or sewing had never appealed. She spent enough time being still when she was running the shop.

Putting Stan down, she selected a book on mountain climbing, then swapped it for one on canoeing. That would be more feasible, given where she lived. She loved watching the canoeists who paddled past *Coralie*, whizzing along and manoeuvring like bicycles on the water.

She sat down with the book, flicking through the pictures of canoeists, and tried to remember if she knew anyone from the local club.

The only name that came to mind was Darwin, which was odd. She'd never met anyone called Darwin. Perhaps Charles Darwin had used a canoe when he visited the Galapagos Islands. An odd image popped into her head: a Victorian caricature of Darwin in a canoe, accompanied by a monkey. She was so tired that she couldn't be sure if she was remembering or imagining it, but at least it was shifting her mind into calmer waters.

She fetched her tablet, entered *Darwin canoe*, and pressed Search.

But top of the results was not Charles Darwin but *John Darwin: the man who faked his own death.*

Stan jumped on her lap and she nearly dropped the tablet. Of course, John Darwin. He'd gone missing in 2002, on a canoe trip out to sea. After the fragments of canoe washed up, he was declared dead. His wife raked in a fortune from the insurance, while in reality, she was hiding him in the house. They might have got away with it if a photograph of them buying property in Panama hadn't been spotted five years later.

Mmm, she thought, as she scrolled through the article. *Anne Darwin didn't have to identify a body but she did appear bereaved, though it says here that her emotions were really guilt and fear. What if Jade's right and Madeline is covering up something similar, but she isn't as good an actress? Thinking back, didn't Madeline say 'And he's left me with this dog', not 'And all I have left of him is this dog'? Although then . . . who is the body? And who are Richard and Madeline Bain? Richard had an IT business, and the neighbour said they kept themselves to themselves. No one's said what Madeline does.*

Fi made another search. She couldn't find the Bains on social media or LinkedIn. Nor could she find much about Richard's IT business. Nothing obvious stood out in a quick search of companies, and none of the articles about his death mentioned a company name, so he might be a sole trader doing freelance or commissioned work. The only photograph of him was a shockingly blurry one in the local paper, which had also been broadcast on *Wyvernshire Tonight*. It was as if Madeline had shown the journalist and instead of letting them scan it properly, had held it not quite steady as they photographed it.

'Maybe they were just cautious,' she murmured to Stan. 'Not everyone likes social media. Some people don't want to leave an electronic footprint. And Richard, being in the business, was more cautious than most.'

Perhaps searching for the Bain house might yield

something.

Fi found it listed on a site that told her it had last been sold in 2003, which was much longer than the few years suggested by the neighbour. Either he was wrong, or they must rent it. But why would wealthy people do that?

Uncertain how to establish when the Bains had started renting it, if indeed they had, Fi searched for rental properties within half a mile of their postcode.

The first house that came up was their cottage. Which had just come back on the market.

CHAPTER 19

Jade sprang awake. It was pitch black. She squeezed her eyes shut, then realised she was too warm. 'It's December,' she grumbled, and put one leg outside the covers.

A few minutes later, her foot was cold. 'Aargh!' She leaned on her elbow, flipped the pillow over and flopped down, wincing at her sore bones.

It was no good. Her mind kept jumping from question to question. *Did someone tamper with Fi's brakes? Was it because of our investigation? What should we do?* Irritated with herself, she reached for her phone. *Hopefully it's later than it feels.*

The display said 5.30.

For heaven's sake. Jade unlocked the phone and scrolled through social media for something to do, but every picture of a car, every happy couple, every landscape drew her back to the case. 'Some help you are,' she muttered. Maybe warm milk would send her to sleep. Then she remembered that Hugo would be asleep on the sofa. *I'll have to be really quiet.*

Using her phone as a torch, she tiptoed to the bedroom door and opened it. She could barely see Hugo, who was curled under a quilt. Carefully, she edged round to the kitchenette, poured milk in a pan, and set it gently on her favourite ring of the small stove. She turned the gas on and pressed the ignition.

Click-click-click. In the silence, it was like machine-gun fire.

'It doesn't matter if you shoot me,' murmured Hugo. 'I've got another life. Several, actually.'

Jade held her breath, waiting for him to settle. Instead, she saw a long, pyjamaed arm stretch beyond the sofa, then heard a yawn. 'Mummy? Why are you up in the middle of the night?'

'Couldn't sleep,' said Jade. 'I'm making warm milk to try and send me off. Sorry.'

'It's all right,' said Hugo. 'Are you worried about the car accident?'

'Just slightly.' She had told Hugo what had happened as soon as she arrived back at the flat. His view had been that it was probably a mechanical failure. If anything, he was more annoyed with the truck driver. 'Let me know if you want me to help track him down,' he had said.

Jade imagined Hugo in a trench coat, brandishing a

magnifying glass. 'Thanks, but we'll manage.'

Hugo shrugged. 'Up to you, but if you change your mind…' And he had changed the subject to who had come in and what they'd bought. 'Here's a list of what I sold. Mindfulness is big.'

'I knew it!' cried Jade. Poring over the bestseller lists with Hugo and compiling a stock order had kept her mind off the day's events for at least an hour.

But it never lasted. Her aching bones were a constant reminder.

'Are you sure you don't want me to find that driver?' Hugo asked, looking rather pathetic in his pyjamas.

'Like I said—' Then Jade realised there was something he could help with. 'Fancy a walk?'

'What, now? It's the middle of the night, Mummy.'

'No, it's nearly six. Besides, it's probably better to go to the place I'm thinking of under cover of darkness.'

Hugo's mouth dropped open. 'Mummy, you don't mean—'

'Yep. Fi and I were on our way to the stone circle when the accident happened. My car's still in the garage, so the only way to get there is to walk. As you're so keen on helping, you can be my bodyguard.'

Hugo's brows knitted. 'I can't believe you're serious.' Then his expression became crafty. 'What if I say no?'

Jade drew herself up to her full height. 'I'll go anyway. My phone's got lots of charge.'

'Absolutely not.' Hugo sat up. 'You're not going alone, Mummy. Especially not after what happened yesterday.' He got to his feet. 'Make us strong coffee and toast while I get dressed.'

***

'Here we are,' Jade said an hour later, illuminating the sign with a torch. 'Hazeby Stone Circle, this way.'

'About time too,' said Hugo. 'Have you ever considered power walking?'

'On an unlit country road? Surprisingly, no. Now come along. We've got a field to cross.' Jade checked her phone battery, which was at a reassuring seventy per cent.

'Why did I agree to this?' said Hugo, trailing behind her.

Crossing the field was much easier the second time. Jade suspected it was a combination of having done it before and not being alone. She stopped, and Hugo nearly walked into her. She could barely see him for coat, scarf, and hat. 'Thanks for coming,' she said.

'You owe me,' he replied. 'Now do get a move on, Mummy.'

By the time they had climbed over the stile and started the approach to the stone circle, the sky had lightened a tiny bit. She could just make out the solid, intimidating shapes of the stones hunkering on the plain.

'It's eerie, isn't it?' said Hugo. 'Have they ever filmed a ghost-hunting programme here? They should.'

'Please don't talk about ghosts,' said Jade. 'Let's go and examine the – the scene. I'm surprised they haven't taped it off.'

'I suppose that means they've finished with it,' said Hugo.

When Jade reached the information board, she shone her torch this way and that. 'No particular tracks in the grass,' she said. 'But it's been a few days. I imagine it's sprung back up. Hopefully someone recorded any unusual tracks at the time.'

'The dry weather won't have helped,' said Hugo.

'No.' Jade took several deep breaths, then walked to the stone altar. 'This is where it happened. He was lying here, and a pile of clothes was on the ground nearby.' She closed her eyes and tried to remember what exactly had been in the pile. She visualised Inspector Acaster picking up the first garment and shaking it out. 'That's odd.'

'That's the understatement of the century,' said Hugo.

'No… The clothes were folded. If you'd murdered someone, would you strip them then take time to put their clothes in a neat little pile? Or would you leg it?'

'I'd leg it, obviously,' said Hugo. 'Also, fingerprints? DNA?'

'Exactly, Watson.'

'I told you I don't want to be Watson.'

'You've got the forensic medical knowledge. That makes you Watson. I wonder… Did they bring the clothes with them?'

'So what was he wearing?' said Hugo. 'Or did they take those clothes away with them?'

'It's possible. Especially if… If they would have identified the victim.'

She heard a gasp. 'So it wasn't who everyone thinks?' said Hugo.

'Maybe not.' Jade shone her torch on the altar. 'The body was neat, too. Feet together, arms by his sides. Did they kill him here, then lift him onto the altar? Or did they bring him in a body bag and arrange him? I w—'

'Hold it right there,' barked a voice Jade wished she didn't know.

Jade whipped round and winced as torchlight hit her in the eye. 'Um, hello?'

The torch wavered as Inspector Acaster walked towards them. 'Saw you two take the turning as I was heading to work,' she remarked. 'Don't tell me, Ms Fitch, you're planning a watercolour series.'

'Nope,' said Jade. 'I was going to come down yesterday with Fi Booker, in daylight, but we were involved in a road accident.'

'Of course you were,' said the inspector. 'Have you reported it? I haven't heard about it, if so.'

'Fi was driving, so I left it to her,' said Jade. 'It's a free country. If I want to walk to the stones with my son, you can't stop me.'

Inspector Acaster inspected Hugo, using her torch. 'You're her son?' she asked, doubt clear in her voice.

'I am, yes,' said Hugo. 'Hugo Fitch. You must be Inspector Acaster. Pleased to meet you.' He extended a gloved hand.

Inspector Acaster regarded the hand for some time, then shook it. 'And your reason for being here is…?'

'I couldn't sleep,' said Jade. 'Too much on my mind. So I decided to come here before opening the shop in case anything sparked a memory. And it has.'

Even in the comparative darkness, she could see how unimpressed Inspector Acaster looked. 'Has it,' she said. Then her expression changed. 'Tell me what you've . . . come up with.'

Jade glanced at Hugo, who nodded. 'It's best you tell the police. Especially after what happened yesterday.'

'Your son appears to be a sensible man,' said Inspector Acaster. 'I've no idea where he got that from.'

'Do you want to hear my theory or not?' asked Jade.

‘Yes,’ said Inspector Acaster. ‘I do.’

For the next few minutes Jade poured out her observations and conjectures, and what Fi had pieced together. When she had finished, she gazed at Inspector Acaster, whose face gave nothing away. ‘Well?’

‘I really don’t know what to say,’ said the inspector.

Jade smiled, and Hugo gave her a little nudge. ‘So you—’

‘What a load of twaddle.’ Inspector Acaster stared at Jade as if she were a particularly large slug in her salad. ‘When Marcus Falconer told me about you two, he more or less said you were the greatest thing since sliced bread. Is a crackpot conspiracy theory the best you can come up with?’

‘You’re the one who reckons Satanists did it,’ Jade shot back. Hugo put a restraining hand on her arm, but she shook it off.

‘It’s a line of enquiry,’ said the inspector, ‘and a strong one. I don’t know what trashy novels you read or what rubbish you watch on TV, but this is real life.’ She continued to stare at Jade. ‘I just – I’m astonished that you have the front to tell me, a police inspector, a tale like that. Who do you think you are?’ Jade opened her mouth to speak, but Inspector Acaster held up a hand. ‘No, I don’t need to hear your bluster. You see, I’ve spent a little time looking into you. And if I were you, I'd keep my head down.'

***

That night, Jade woke suddenly. She had slept badly, probably because she had spent the day hiding in the flat while Hugo minded the shop.

Fi had sent a garbled text at around 8am, which Jade hadn't seen till she woke from a fitful sleep mid-morning. She frowned at it, then replied *I have to stay out of this* and switched off her phone. Not even a Chinese takeaway with Hugo had managed to pull her out of the doldrums.

She pulled the covers over her head. *So long as I keep out of this, I'll be safe. Inspector Acaster won't do anything to me if I behave myself. And once Marcus Falconer gets back, she'll be out of the picture. I've just got to hold on.*

The clock ticked in the silence, and she considered taking the battery out. She became aware of a faint noise. A sort of whooshing, but very quiet. *Maybe it's a pigeon outside. A big pigeon. Or an escaped pheasant? Is it the right season?*

Another faint whoosh, and a sort of ticking. Not like the clock. Irregular.

Jade threw off the covers and listened. As she did so, her nose twitched. *What's that smell?* It was . . . petrol? *Has a car broken down?*

Then she realised. She leapt out of bed, grabbed her phone, and thundered downstairs.

When she opened the door that led to the shop, she gasped. Flames licked at the carpet, making shadows dance on the walls. Cold air hit her from the hole in the shattered window. And in the middle of it all, a broken bottle rolled on the floor.

CHAPTER 20

I have to stay out of this. Jade's dismissive response didn't come until over two hours after Fi had sent her message about the canoe case.

What does she want, exactly? thought Fi, her fingers hovering. *First she wants me to prove she didn't commit murder, then she ghosts me, then she wants my help. She tells me my car's been tampered with, and now she wants to drop it. No explanation. How does she think that makes me feel? I'm not a book to be picked up or dropped, depending on her mood. How would she feel if I did that to her?*

Fi felt her jaw clench. *We're on to something and I don't want to work it out without her, but there's no choice. She'll probably sulk, and then she'll leave... I'd miss her if she left. I wish she'd explain why her default response is to run away. Doesn't she trust me? I've trusted her with stuff hardly anyone knows.*

She put the phone face down on the table before she sent a message she'd regret later, and put the kettle on. The phone vibrated as a new message came in.

'You'll have to wait,' she muttered, jotting down ideas about what to do – alone – on a piece of paper. Ring the garage, for a start. Cycle out to the stones next. Do a bit more digging into the Bains. Then there was the body. If it wasn't Richard Bain, who was it? Was it possible to find the names of recently missing people online?

Fi paused as she wrote. She wished, in a way, that she'd seen the victim's injuries in daylight. She grimaced, unable to remember them clearly.

The phone vibrated again. This time, she turned it over.

The message wasn't from Jade but her friend Carla. *Are you OK? Am I waiting in the wrong place?*

'Oh flip,' said Fi. She typed *I'll be there in five mins* and knocked on Dylan's door. Hearing a grunt, she poked her head round. 'I'm off out. Can you look after Stan? I'll be back this afternoon.'

'Wha—?' yawned Dylan. 'Has Jade found another body?'

'Not that I know of,' said Fi. 'I'm visiting a modern art exhibition in Spetisham with Carla. I'd forgotten we'd arranged it, to be honest. If, er… If Jade does turn up, tell her to ring me, OK? Oh, and you remember the kid from your school who ran away last year? How did the police publicise it?'

'Is this a different investigation?' Dylan managed to say, in the middle of another yawn. 'Are you asking me to help?'

'Kind of.'

'Can't remember. But it wasn't just the police that helped find her. I'll have a think.'

'Thanks,' said Fi. 'Tell me when you can. And let me know if you're going out. Keep the place locked up and don't eat everything.'

'Yeah, whatever.' Dylan snuggled under the covers as Stan slinked in. Fi suspected he'd jump on Dylan's bed as soon as she was gone. There wasn't time to intervene.

Fi went to change and put make-up on. It would be good to get out of the town for a bit and concentrate on something completely different. Things might become clearer. And perhaps, by the time she got back, Jade would have been in touch.

'I thought maybe you were busy poking around in that murder and you'd forgotten,' said Carla, when Fi arrived at the car park. She didn't wait for an answer. 'Or are you taking a day off? I can't even do Wordle, I'd be rubbish at a real problem. Anyway, I'm glad you can come.'

'Need some culture?'

'Need to get away from the kids. Can we sue the

person who invented teenagers? At least when I laugh at the weird art you won't tell me that I don't understand post-ironic modernism, or that I'm proof of the inherent wotsit of Generation X, or whatever. Does Jade want to come? Oh, I suppose she's got the shop open.'

'Yup,' said Fi, without the remotest idea.

'Shame. I'd love to hear Jade's opinions of modern art. And she could do with getting away from gossiping scumballs for a bit. As if Jade's shop has anything to do with a murder.'

'Exactly.'

'Anyway, how was Christmas? Man, it was a trial for me. I told Tom that next year we're going abroad, just him, me and the kids. If he doesn't like it, he can stay home with his mum.'

Fi laughed and managed to get a few sentences in before Carla was off again. Her mind disconnected from the murder as she listened to Carla describing the near-incineration of a vegan alternative main, the teenager who'd demanded it and the mother-in-law who'd complained about it. A weight lifted the further they got from town.

She came home as the sun was setting and popped into the garage.

'Sorry, love,' said George. 'We're sorting out your friend's Volvo. It's like raising the dead, but don't tell her. Your insurance have asked us to source you a courtesy car. It's the Fiat 500 over there.' He handed her the keys and contemplated her height. 'If you get in, I hope you make it out.'

When she arrived home, Dylan had gone to the theatre. He'd left a list of websites and a drawing of a haystack with the words *Find the needle* next to it.

Fi took Stan for a short walk, then prepared dinner. Afterwards, she did some more research and found a programme to watch on TV until Dylan came home, when she went to bed.

At one in the morning she was jerked from a dreamless sleep by fire-engine sirens. *What's going on?*

She crept out of bed and went on deck to look towards the town. The sirens had stopped, but the sky appeared to flicker. Was it smoke, or her imagination? Should she get dressed and head down? *And be one of those people who get in the way,* she chided herself. She opened the local Facebook page, but the posts were about parking charges, lost mobiles, and teenagers on e-scooters. One post mentioned sirens but no one had answered. Then again, it was the middle of the night. Perhaps she'd dreamed it.

She hesitated, then messaged Jade. *I thought I heard fire engines. Are you OK?*

There was some wibbling, followed by *Am OK.*

Fi went back to bed, unsure if her sense of unease was due to the sirens or her failure to discover anything useful. She drifted into a shallow sleep and was woken at two am by another message from Jade.

Am OK but at police station, in the witness suite.

Fi blinked and hit Reply. *What?*

Someone set fire to the shop. We've been evacuated and they've taken statements and they're finding clothes for us before we work out where to go.

Why didn't you say? Why didn't you come here?

Didn't want to bother you.

Oh Jade. For pity's sake. I'll come and get you.

At the police station, Fi was escorted to the witness suite and found Jade and Hugo in pyjamas, wrapped in blankets. Hugo was busy on his laptop, his usually amiable face darkened by a scowl.

Jade looked up. 'How did you get here? Is your car fixed?'

'They haven't even started on it yet,' said Fi, sitting down next to her. 'So I don't know if there's something odd about the brakes. I've got a courtesy car.'

Jade grunted.

'The brakes?' asked the officer who'd escorted her. 'Are you the one who went in that ditch?'

'That's me,' said Fi. 'An idiot was on the wrong side of the road and forced me to take evasive action. He ought to be prosecuted, and my insurance company needed a crime number. But my brakes weren't working: I should have been able to stop sooner. Although…' She swallowed. 'I'd have had to stop at some point, and if… Anyway.'

The constable looked from her to Jade. 'Right, I'll see what's happening on that. When you're ready, my colleague will let you out of the other exit.'

Fi touched Jade's arm. The stench of smoke wafted from her hair. 'What happened?'

'A Molotov cocktail through the front door,' said Jade.

'What?'

'I must have been woken by the smash. When I went downstairs, the carpet was on fire and it was spreading to the display in the window. Luckily, the fire extinguisher was to hand. I put the fire out and Hugo phoned for help. But there's some plastic stuff in my stock, so the place reeks. And it's an old building, so the fire could still be smouldering somewhere. They had to evacuate Rick too, as a precaution. I must be the worst neighbour ever.'

'Oh my goodness.' Fi went to hug Jade, but she fended her off.

'Don't, I smell awful. They wouldn't let us fetch any clothes, though Hugo managed to sneak his laptop out.'

'Because they're worried the building might be dangerous?'

'That, and because they need to see what caused the fire if it wasn't the obvious.'

A police officer arrived and handed Jade and Hugo a small pile each: jeans, T-shirt, a sweater. Both grimaced, their individual styles about to be anonymised. 'The showers are through there.' The constable pointed down a corridor. 'Then we'll get you to the Crown Hotel, if you've nowhere else. The force has an arrangement with them for emergency victim accommodation.'

Jade sagged in her chair.

'Surely you know I'll put you up?' said Fi. 'Come as you are, and you can shower on the boat. There's the sofa bed in the aft for one of you and the sofa in the main shop for the other. I have plenty of spare bedding.'

Jade exchanged glances with Hugo.

'Come on, Mummy,' he said. 'We'll be among friends, and at least no one but Fi will see us dressed in such an average way at breakfast. Tomorrow is another day.'

'Oh, all right,' said Jade. She gave Fi a wonky smile. 'Thanks.'

They left the building and made their way to the car.

'I hope the flat's not still a crime scene tomorrow,' said Jade glumly, after she'd folded herself into the Fiat. Hugo was already squished up in the back, a contorted picture of gloom.

'The flat won't be, surely,' said Fi, starting the

engine. 'Is there much damage up there?'

'The damage is to the shop,' said Jade. 'And that's mostly smoke damage. But working out if it really was a crime, and if so, whether it was someone from outside, might involve going through my stuff.'

'What do you…' Fi took in Jade's weary, defeated expression. 'They can't suspect you did it yourself?'

'Can't they? I increased my contents insurance a few weeks ago because I have more valuable stock in Crystal Dreams now. People commit crimes to claim off the insurance all the time.'

'Some people do. *You* wouldn't,' said Fi. 'Funnily enough, that's what I was trying to talk to you about yesterday. What if—'

'Forget it. I've tried to tell the police what we've worked out and they're not listening. Let them do their job.'

'But someone is dead,' said Fi. 'We have to keep going. If you don't want to help, I respect that, but I'll do it on my own.'

'You can't!'

'I can,' said Fi. 'I'm not putting up with having my brakes cut and your place attacked, and letting whoever it is get away with it. I'm carrying on regardless.'

CHAPTER 21

Jade woke to the sound of small morning noises – the quiet roar of a boiling kettle, the chink of cutlery. She could tell even without opening her eyes that it had started to get light.

Is Hugo up? He's never up first. She opened her eyes and was confronted by an unfamiliar pillow. Then she remembered.

'Morning,' said Fi. She was still in pyjamas and dressing gown. 'Sorry if I woke you.'

'What time is it?' Jade looked at her phone. Half past seven. 'I didn't think I'd sleep a wink.'

'I imagine you needed it,' said Fi. 'I haven't checked on Hugo yet. I'd send Dylan, but he won't stir for hours.' She sat on the edge of the sofa bed. 'How are you feeling?'

Jade blinked as she considered the question. The first word that came to mind was *hopeless*, and she dismissed it as pathetic and needy. But really… No shop, no home, in the middle of winter? 'I've felt better,' she said.

Fi gave her a quick hug. 'I'm sure you have, but hopefully this is temporary. You'll be back in the shop and your flat before you know it. I'll make you a strong cup of tea and some toast. That always helps. Why don't you shower while I do that?'

Jade did as she was told, then changed into what she thought of as her prison uniform. The jeans were loose at the waist, tight on the hips, and two inches too short, while the T-shirt was a size too small. She scrubbed her head with a towel and gave a hank of hair an experimental sniff. *At least it isn't smoky.* But when she glanced in the mirror she didn't look like herself at all. She stomped out of the bathroom and sat down at the galley table, where Hugo, in his pyjamas, was frowning at his laptop.

'Hugo, really?' she said. 'I'm sure whatever you're doing can wait.'

'It's fine,' said Fi, not turning from the worktop where she was buttering rounds of toast. 'I've subcontracted.'

As a response, Hugo angled the laptop to face her. She peered at it. 'What the—?'

On the screen was a photograph of the truck driver who had almost crashed into Fi's car. 'How did you…?'

'I asked Fi a couple of questions and had a little dig around,' said Hugo. 'Pete Jameson, forty-seven, lives at 1 Church Cottages. Self employed as a tree surgeon. Divorced, two grown-up kids. Truck registration—'

'Good grief.' Jade held up her hands to stop the flow of information. 'Have you got his inside leg measurement, too?'

'Not yet.' Hugo grinned. 'But I can give you his mobile number. He doesn't have a landline.'

Jade took this in. 'So now we know who he is, we can report him to the police for dangerous driving.'

'You could,' said Hugo, with a distinct twinkle in his eye. 'Or we could make his life a living hell. Send him on fake tree-surgery expeditions all over Wyvernshire. Block his mobile. That sort of thing.'

'Scary, isn't it,' said Fi, delivering two mugs of tea and a big plate of toast. 'I've got marmalade or blackcurrant jam. Help yourself.'

'At least that's one mystery solved,' said Jade. 'Thanks, Hugo.' The first sip of tea was heavenly. 'Turns out all that education is good for something.'

'About solving mysteries…' Fi took the third seat at the table, a folding one. 'Since you've got time on your hands at the moment, Jade…'

Jade sighed. 'But I can't think straight. I'm too worried. What if it takes months to get the shop put right? What if all my stock's damaged? And what if the police won't let us into the flat? We can't sleep on your sofas for the next month.'

Fi sipped her drink and set it on the coaster with a decisive clack. 'Firstly, you could if you had to. Secondly, you're catastrophising, because you told me yesterday it wasn't too bad. Thirdly, I can help you with the insurance stuff. I'm good at bureaucracy. And even if the shop's closed for a while, you can sell your undamaged stock in the Book Barge.'

'Thanks, Fi. I do appreciate it. I'll feel better when I know the situation.'

'So go down when you've had your breakfast, Mummy,' said Hugo.

Fi grinned. 'The boy speaks truth.'

'There's no need to gang up on me,' Jade replied, but she couldn't help smiling. 'Honestly, a woman can't wallow in despair for two minutes round here without someone intervening.'

'Yep,' said Fi, and took a piece of toast. 'I suggest you eat this before it goes rubbery.'

After breakfast, Jade borrowed a coat from Fi and set off for Crystal Dreams. She'd invited Hugo, but he had said firmly that he would rather stay indoors. 'Although if you could bring me back a decent outfit, Mummy…'

Jade rolled her eyes. 'I'll see what I can do.'

As she drew nearer to the shop, she noticed a knot of people standing in the street, all facing the same way. Some were on tiptoe. *Bet I know what they're looking at*, she thought, and her spirits plummeted.

A couple of them turned as she approached. She recognised one of the three witches, though she was less well-groomed than usual. 'It's terrible, Jade, absolutely terrible,' she said, and put a hand on Jade's arm. 'You poor thing. Were you there when it happened?'

'I was,' said Jade. 'Luckily, it woke me. I put the fire out with an extinguisher and my son rang 999.'

'Thank heavens,' she breathed. 'You must have *sensed* danger.'

'Jade!' Netta came running up. 'What the heck?'

'Petrol bomb,' said Jade. 'Spent the rest of the night at Fi's.'

Netta gaped. 'Will we have to close?'

Jade bit back her first response. 'I should think so,' she said. 'If they'll let me in, I can assess the damage.'

With a lot of excuse-mes and tactical use of elbows, she got herself to the front of the crowd. A police officer was guarding the door. 'No gawkers,' he said sternly.

'It's my shop,' Jade told him. 'And I live upstairs.'

'Wait here.' He opened the door and went inside.

Jade looked through the broken window. He was talking to Inspector Acaster, who glanced outside and rolled her eyes.

The police officer returned. 'Don't touch anything,' he said, and held the door open for her.

Jade stepped carefully in. Two officers in white overalls were chatting in a corner, and the area behind the window was cordoned off with police tape. 'Are you the owner?' one of the officers asked.

Jade nodded, suddenly unable to speak. In the cold light of day, the shop looked terrible. The midnight-blue walls were streaked with dark grey and scorched concrete showed through the hole in the carpet, which smelt of burning, wet dog and fire-extinguisher chemicals. Most of the stock in the window was beyond saving, except for the remaining geode, which stood proudly in the centre.

'It's a bit of a mess.' Jade jumped. Inspector Acaster had materialised next to her.

'You know when I said Fi and I were on to something…?'

The inspector shrugged. 'Maybe someone just doesn't like your shop. A religious person or a sceptic, maybe.'

'Mmm. But when you add that to Fi's car accident… Her brakes failed. A month after she'd had the car serviced.'

Inspector Acaster said nothing for some time. 'If you want to collect a few clothes and essentials from your flat, you may,' she said eventually. 'I'll need to see what you've taken, though. The fire service investigation team have to finish before giving me a report. They haven't gone up there yet: they've been too busy with the shop.'

'Thanks.' Jade headed for the connecting door, then paused. 'When will I be able to come back in?'

Inspector Acaster beckoned one of the suited-up officers, who came over. 'When will you be finished, Ted?'

'Shouldn't be long,' he replied. 'We've gathered what we can of the bottle and its contents for fingerprinting and analysis. Whoever did it clearly didn't enter the shop: the hole in the window's too small. So yeah, you could be in later today.' A gust of cold air ruffled his overalls and he shivered. 'Whether you'd want to is another matter.'

'I've seen plenty worse,' said Inspector Acaster, and Jade stared at her. Was the inspector actually being – not nice exactly, but not actively horrible? 'Can this lady go upstairs for some of her personal belongings from the flat?'

'Yes,' said Ted. 'Ms Fitch, I suggest you contact your insurance company, if you haven't already. The inspector can give you the crime number.'

Jade's legs were heavy as she climbed the stairs. She imagined phone calls, paperwork, more phone calls, sending and resending photographs of the damage. She entered the flat, which bewilderingly looked the same as ever, and bundled two changes of clothes for herself and Hugo in a bag, along with basic toiletries and a proper bra. Just handling her own things made her feel better. She held a velvet top to her cheek. It calmed her, like stroking a cat.

'Clothes and toiletries,' she said to Inspector Acaster downstairs, and held the bag open for her inspection.

The inspector moved a few items aside. 'OK. We'll contact you when we're finished. I assume you have your phone.'

'Yes,' said Jade. *Now to go to Fi's and twiddle my thumbs, I suppose…* A thought struck her. 'Can I get my notebook, please? It's in the counter drawer.'

'Your notebook?' Inspector Acaster frowned. 'What's in it?'

'Stock information, customers, phone numbers… Business stuff. For the insurance claim.'

'Yeah, OK.' She sounded bored. Perhaps not being horrible was hard work for her.

Jade popped behind the counter and retrieved the book. 'Thanks again,' she said, and went on her way.

She smiled as she crossed *Coralie*'s gangplank. *There's bound to be something in the notebook that will help us*. By the time she entered the boat, she was positively beaming. But when she called 'I'm back, and I've got the notebook,' there was no response.

She froze. *They can't have gone out. They wouldn't have left the boat unlocked*. 'Hello?'

‘Jade, we’re in the galley,’ Fi called. ‘Come and see this.’

A shiver went down Jade’s spine, something which, until recently, she had thought only happened in books. She walked slowly towards the galley, wondering what was waiting for her.

CHAPTER 22

Jade, clasping a large bag to her front as if afraid it would escape, looked desperate for tea. Hugo enveloped both her and the bag with his long arms, kissed the top of her head, released her to kiss a cherry-red sweater in the bag, and put the kettle on.

'What do I have to come and see?' said Jade.

'Your son's a genius,' said Fi. 'If a slightly dubious one.'

'Like mother, like son,' said Jade, relaxing a little.

'Of course.' Fi patted the seat beside her. 'Now you're here, I can explain why I think so, and he can go out and order hot brunch rolls from Willow's Wagon. We need more than toast to work on.'

'Can't I change first?' said Hugo, clasping the sweater.

Fi rolled her eyes. 'Hugo, we're starving, and it'll take Willow a while to cook anything. Can you order wearing what you've got on now? Then you can pop back and dress at your leisure. All Willow's stuff is organic, and she has plant-based alternatives.'

'Oh, very well,' said Hugo. 'One shall be a blur, and hopefully no one will realise these are supermarket jeans.'

'Jeans are all the same to me,' said Jade, as he rushed out. 'I hate them. Give me a skirt any day. In fact—'

'How were things at the shop?'

'A crowd a mile deep. The fire investigation team's there, and so are the police. Inspector Acaster was…'

'Annoying? Bossy? Unsympathetic?'

'The first two, yes, but the last… She was actually trying to be sympathetic. I imagine it hurt.' Jade managed a small smile.

'Try not to worry too much,' said Fi. 'Whatever else she is, I think she's on the level. You've nothing to hide, and I don't believe she'd plant anything on you. And I'm not your only friend in town, Jade. We'll sort things out with your shop and home somehow, I promise. Not today, obviously. But soon.'

Jade's smile grew a little broader and she rubbed the corner of her eye. 'Go on then, why is my son a genius?'

'Look at this.'

'What?' Jade reached for the bag and held it tight like an oversized teddy bear.

'This.' Fi turned Hugo's laptop so that they could both see it. 'I'm glad he used his own, not mine. Not that I'd have a clue where to look. Or *how* to look.'

'Look at what?'

Fi lowered her voice. 'Hugo went on the dark web.'

Jade's mouth dropped open. The kettle boiled and Fi got up to make drinks. Jade glanced at Dylan's cabin door.

'He's asleep,' said Fi. 'But I bet he'll wake as soon as he smells brunch. I don't mind if he overhears what Hugo found, just not how he found it.' She put their mugs down and moved the mouse to stop the laptop from locking. A photograph of Richard Bain appeared. He was posing in a sharp suit, arms folded. It wasn't blurry like the one in the papers, but he appeared twenty years younger. 'This is his business site. His *other* business site, Get Rich Quick.'

'Other business site?' Jade peered at the screen. 'It still says IT expert. What's the difference? Why be on the' – she lowered her voice to a whisper – 'the dark web?'

'Because the services are different. Look.' Fi clicked. The terminology was vague, legitimate-sounding, mentioning assistance with investment strategies and deep-dives into interested parties' software. *Discretion guaranteed.*

Jade read, frowning a little. 'Money laundering? Hacking?'

'Yup,' said Fi.

'So the body *is* his? Someone suspects that he's behind their system being hacked and… But surely they wouldn't bother with all that sacrifice rigmarole?'

'I don't think it's his body,' said Fi. 'Hugo found this, too.'

She clicked on another tab. It was a thread where someone was not only seeking information about Richard Bain, but seeking the man himself. Apparently, money had been laundered through an account and most had never re-emerged. 'They're convinced someone has siphoned off money, and the finger of suspicion points firmly at the person who coded those dodgy digital transactions: Richard Bain.'

'It's more than a finger of suspicion,' said Jade, scrolling. 'It's a downright accusation. If they do catch up with him, they won't waste time with words. Look at the reward they're offering to anyone who knows his whereabouts! I could buy the whole of the high street with that, fill it with golden cauldrons, and still have change to buy you a yacht and a Caribbean island to moor it off.'

'I don't think they *have* caught up with him.' Hugo stepped into the galley and grabbed the bag of clothes. 'If you carry on scrolling and check the other tabs, it's clear they couldn't track him down, and they're pretty disgusted that he's dead because they can't sort him out themselves. But there's nothing to indicate that anyone has murdered him, despite this being the sort of place where someone might be happy enough to say they'd killed him and how. They're not the sort of people who are shy about their skills.' Hugo shuddered. 'I'm not finding you the photos to prove it. Right, I'm popping to the aft to change. A man's sartorial needs come first. *À bientôt*.'

'Wouldn't they go after Madeline Bain?' said Jade, once he'd gone.

'Not if Richard had given them the impression that any capital was out of her reach,' said Fi. 'Or that she didn't know where his wealth came from. There are no other family members to threaten, either. All he needs to do is disappear and his problems will disappear too. Then he can pop up elsewhere and access money which he's doubtless hidden under a false name. Which begs a load of questions. Was Madeline unaware of the money and did she believe the body was his? Or did she know about the money and believe the body was his? Or did she know about the money and identify another man's body to cover Richard's disappearance, which makes her complicit?'

'I think she's complicit,' said Jade. 'So who is the dead man and which of them killed him? And why dump him at the stones with those clothes beside him?'

Hugo returned in the cherry-red sweater, navy chinos and highly polished tan brogues. 'I'm fit to collect brunch. Then we can dig a bit more.'

Before Fi could answer, her phone rang.

The call was from the garage. 'Hello?' said the owner. He sounded anxious. 'Is that Fi? It's George.'

'Hi. Yes, it's me. Have you had the chance to look at my car?'

'I have. Can you walk me through what happened again?'

Fi mouthed *garage* at Jade. She was tempted to put the phone on speaker, but was conscious that Dylan's cabin was feet away and he might be awake. She walked out of the galley and into the wheelhouse, with Jade following. 'I was driving normally and not especially fast along the Monkton road. When I approached that sharp bend, someone was coming the other way but on my side of the road. I braked, the brakes seemed spongy, there was a strange smell and… I was steering to the left anyway, but the car oversteered into the ditch.'

'Did you see the brake light come on?'

'Not beforehand,' said Fi. 'At the time, I was too busy avoiding the pickup to watch the dashboard.'

'Any fluid under the car recently?'

'What sort of fluid? Oil?'

'Not oil. Nearly clear viscous stuff.'

'I hadn't noticed. The car was in the car park and

it's been raining recently.'

'Not under the car it hasn't.'

'No, but I don't use it that often. And it's mostly been dark. I might have spotted a patch of oil as I was pulling away, maybe. But nothing else. Even if I'd looked.'

George made a noise that combined despair of anyone who didn't inspect their vehicle every day with worry.

'You're talking about brake fluid, aren't you?' She heard her voice quaver and Jade patted her arm.

Hugo entered the wheelhouse from outside, bearing a tray with wrapped rolls and sandwiches, gave them a quizzical glance, then descended into the boat. Savoury smells wafted as he passed, but Fi's appetite had gone.

'Yeah, I'm talking about brake fluid,' said George. 'One of the lines has been cut. It must have leaked for a while, but maybe you didn't clock it. You'd never have known till the brake failed. All I can say is I'm glad you didn't get forced into oncoming traffic. Not that it couldn't have been… I mean—' George cleared his throat. 'The thing is, Fi, it wasn't like that when it was here for service. And it looks deliberate, not accidental. Whoever did it hacked at it, so I suspect they weren't one hundred per cent sure what they were doing. You must tell the police, if you haven't already.'

‘I have, but all they’ll do is check for marks on the road to see if the pickup driver was at fault. If they’ve even done that.’

‘Well, they’d better get cracking, and more importantly, they need to hear about this. What with that bloke at the stones, and this, and your pal’s shop was set on fire too… I reckon a maniac’s out there. Tell the police, Fi. They can come and inspect it any time. And stay safe, love.’

Fi ended the call and stared at Jade. Before she could say anything, a message arrived from Marcus.

Heard about Jade’s place. What’s going on? Take care, Fi. Trust your instincts, but know when you need an expert.

‘What did the garage say?’ said Jade.

‘You were right about the brakes.’

‘We must tell Hugo before the smell of brunch wakes Dylan,’ said Jade. But she wasn’t smiling.

They hurried into the galley and Jade whispered in Hugo’s ear. He looked at Fi, aghast, then opened his laptop. ‘Right. Time for more digging.’

‘No,’ said Fi. ‘This has to stop, but it needs more than just us to do it. If the inspector won’t listen, we’ll go higher. Either way, we’re going to the police and we’re going now.’

‘Can it be now plus five minutes?’ said Jade. ‘I’ve got to change into my own clothes. If I have to argue with that woman, I need all the confidence I can get.’

CHAPTER 23

'Come on, you two!' Hugo ran down the high street, turning every so often to urge on Jade and Fi. 'We haven't a minute to— Oh, I'm so sorry!' He reached out for the arm of the person he had run into. As Jade caught up, she saw that it was Netta.

'Sorry, Netta, no time to talk,' she gasped. 'I see you've met Hugo.'

Netta stared at Hugo. She didn't seem particularly impressed. 'This is Hugo?'

'That's me,' said Hugo. 'I'm terribly sorry for bumping into you, but I'm afraid we're in a hurry.' He hadn't let go of her arm. 'So you're Netta? *The* Netta?'

Netta laughed. 'The one and only.'

'This is very nice,' said Fi, 'but may I remind you what we're supposed to be doing?' She jerked a thumb at the shop. The police officer was no longer stationed outside, but the two officers in overalls appeared to be packing up. 'Come on.'

Jade knocked and one of the officers opened the door. 'You must be psychic,' he said, with a smile. 'Another ten minutes and we'll be out of your way.'

'Is Inspector Acaster still there?'

He laughed. 'Want to know if the coast is clear, do you? She returned to the station a quarter of an hour ago.'

Jade didn't wait to reply. 'To the station!' she cried, and hurried back the way they had come, almost mowing Netta down in the process.

***

'We need to talk to Inspector Acaster,' said Fi.

The desk sergeant blinked. 'She's not available. Can I ask what it's concerning?'

'You can.' Jade leaned across the counter and he drew back a little. 'A murder,' she muttered.

'I'm sure she's in a meeting,' he countered.

'She may be,' said Jade. 'But I'm pretty sure that if Inspector Falconer were here, he'd see us. Meeting or no meeting.'

The officer thought this over. 'I'll give her a ring,' he said, at last. 'Like I said, though, she's busy.' He picked up the desk phone and prodded the keypad slowly. Then he motioned them away from the counter. 'Take a seat, why don't you.'

'Do you think she'll come out?' Hugo whispered.

'No idea,' Jade whispered back. 'After all that niceness earlier, she might be regenerating in her coffin.'

'Oh, Mummy.' Hugo looked disappointed.

The desk sergeant cleared his throat. 'The inspector will come and collect you in a few minutes.'

Jade and Fi exchanged glances. 'Maybe we're VIPs now,' said Jade. But when Inspector Acaster entered the waiting area, her expression was less suggestive of a warm welcome than of facing the inevitable.

'Thank you for meeting us at such short notice,' Fi said, as they followed her down the corridor.

'In here, please,' the inspector replied, opening the door of a room labelled *INTERVIEW ROOM TWO*. They entered, and she moved a chair so that three seats faced one. 'Take a seat. And before you say anything, I'm only seeing you to get it over with. The last thing I need is you three causing a scene in the station.'

'We wouldn't do that,' said Fi.

'Mmm,' said Inspector Acaster. 'Well, go on then. Out with it.' She put the document she was carrying face down on the table. 'I've got an interesting report to finish reading.'

'Is it anything to do with the case?' Jade asked. She eyed the document, but the paper was too thick to see through.

'I'm sure you're aware that's none of your

business,' said the inspector. 'Please don't waste my time.'

'We have new information about Richard Bain,' said Jade. 'Information that has a huge bearing on the case.' What could that document be? Suddenly, it clicked. 'If, as I suspect, that's the post-mortem report…' Inspector Acaster's eyes narrowed. Strangely, Jade found that more comforting than dealing with the sympathetic version. 'Anything . . . unexpected in there?'

'The whole point of a post-mortem is that it's performed when the death is unexpected,' said Inspector Acaster. 'If that's all you've come here for—'

'I'd bet good money that it isn't the body of Richard Bain,' said Jade. Under the desk, Hugo's hand found hers and squeezed it.

'I am not at liberty to discuss a confidential document with you,' said the inspector.

'In that case…' Jade stood up. 'I suppose we can't share our information either. Shame. Come on, you two. If we crack on, maybe we can get someone to board up the shop window.'

'Wait!' The word rang out like a gunshot. Inspector Acaster stared at Jade. 'Sit down. This had better be good.'

'Oh, it is,' said Hugo, and Jade squeezed his hand back. 'But if you want to hear it, I'm afraid you'll have to go first.'

Behind the inspector's stony facade, Jade imagined her emotions. Anger, definitely. Frustration, probably. But also, there would be curiosity.

After perhaps half a minute, Inspector Acaster flipped over the report and folded her arms. 'Nothing I'm about to say goes outside this room.'

'Of course not,' said Fi. 'We wouldn't dream of it.'

The inspector glared at each of them in turn. 'I'm perfectly capable of making your lives a living hell,' she said, and Jade believed her.

'Right. Well… The findings of the post-mortem are, to say the least, odd. Firstly, the head injuries were inflicted after death. The only possible exception to this, because it's impossible to tell, is the extensive damage to the victim's teeth.'

'Dental records,' murmured Jade.

The inspector continued as if she had not spoken. 'There were high levels of alcohol in the blood, which might point to a verdict of misadventure. However, there were also very high levels of antihistamine. So much so that it's unlikely the victim could have reached the stone circle unaided.'

'But unless he had severe allergies…' said Fi.

'Antihistamine is also present in several over-the-counter sleep aids,' said Inspector Acaster.

'Oh,' said Hugo. 'Thank you for that information, Inspector.'

She narrowed her eyes at him. 'The report also highlights that the victim was malnourished and almost certainly had a history of substance abuse. This doesn't fit with our picture of Mr Bain. Certainly not according to his wife's statement, at any rate.'

'Because it wasn't him!' said Jade. 'Now we can tell you the motive. It's—'

'Just a moment,' said Inspector Acaster, and switched on the tape recorder.

***

After a couple of sentences, Jade noticed that the inspector had a dangerous gleam in her eye, like a cat about to pounce on a bird. She glanced at Fi. 'Fi, will you take over?'

'Certainly.' As Fi talked, Inspector Acaster's shoulders became marginally less stiff. She still frowned from time to time, but occasionally she nodded.

Fi handed over to Hugo for the dark-web narrative, which Hugo kept mercifully short. 'I run a small tech company, Inspector, so sometimes I can spot things which are . . . let's say out of the ordinary. I can send you screenshots of the information we found, and if I had my laptop with me, I could show you in person.'

'I think we have enough to go on,' said Inspector Acaster, and stopped the tape recorder. 'But I have to say, that was most interesting.'

A compliment! Jade hoped the warm feeling

coursing through her wasn't apparent to the inspector. 'So what happens next?' she asked.

'We have to act quickly,' said Inspector Acaster. 'Warrants to access the Bains' technology and their bank accounts. We'll bring Mrs Bain in for more questioning, but not yet.'

'What?' cried Jade. 'What if she does a runner?'

Inspector Acaster smiled. 'I doubt that will happen. First she has to bury her "husband", and that won't happen immediately. Plus if there's a life insurance payout on the way, she'll wait for that.'

'OK,' said Jade. 'What do you want us to do?'

Inspector Acaster looked her straight in the eye. 'Stay out of it.'

Jade's mouth dropped open. 'You're kidding me.'

'I'm not.' Inspector Acaster leaned forward, elbows on the table. The gesture was completely at odds with her sharp suit. 'If your theory is correct, the Bains have already attempted to kill or at least harm both of you. I strongly suggest you leave this to the professionals.'

'The inspector has a point, Mummy,' said Hugo. 'We've moved the case on, but now things must be done officially. Rubber-stamped.'

'Quite.' The inspector stood up. 'I need to set the wheels in motion.' She led the way out of the room and took them part-way down the corridor. 'If you go to the end, that door leads to the reception area.' She felt in her jacket pocket and handed them each a business card. 'If you have any further information related to the case, or if either of the Bains are threatening you, call me. The mobile is always on.'

'Thank you,' they chorused.

At the end of the corridor, Jade looked back. Inspector Acaster walked with long strides, head held high. *I actually hope she catches them.*

She nudged Fi. 'Are you all right?'

'Relieved,' said Fi, with a smile. 'I know you wanted the glory of catching the Bains, but I must admit that a few weeks – a few months – of peace and quiet would be absolutely wonderful.'

Jade grinned. 'I hate to admit it, but I know exactly what you mean. Let's go home.' She opened the door and entered the reception, then gasped. At the counter, waiting, was Madeline Bain. She backtracked, cannoning into Fi. 'Quick, go back!'

'Ow!' Fi glared at her. 'What are you doing?'

Madeline Bain glanced their way. Jade turned and walked Fi into the corridor by the shoulders. 'It's *her*!'

Fi's eyes widened. 'Oh no! Has she seen us?'

Jade slumped against the wall. 'I don't know.'

CHAPTER 29

If Madeline Bain had stayed put, they might have got away. But as Jade and Fi entered the car park, having obtained permission to use an alternative exit, Fi glanced over her shoulder and saw Madeline in the doorway of the station, looking out. Her gaze found Jade and Fi.

They were some distance apart, and winter gloom made faces hard to see. Fi hoped it made them difficult to identify. On the other hand, with her long swirling skirt and purple jacket, Jade wasn't exactly inconspicuous.

Apparently deep in thought, Hugo walked past Madeline, then Fi and Jade, with no acknowledgement. He stopped beside a VW Touran and started tapping on his phone.

Fortunately, Fi's courtesy car was in a lower tier, out of Madeline's line of vision. 'Quick,' whispered

Fi. 'Once we're past these steps, phone Hugo and tell him to stay put. Madeline's watching us. Ask him to tell us when she goes back in.'

'OK.' Jade rang Hugo as they scurried down the steps and they hid behind a Toyota Sequoia, in case Madeline decided to follow them. 'He twigged, which is why he pretended not to be with us. He's going inside and he'll let us know when she does the same. If she leaves, he'll tail her. He's a resourceful lad.'

'He's not so resourceful that he can keep up with a car on foot,' said Fi. 'He could borrow a police bicycle, if there's still such a thing.'

'Not in those trousers,' said Jade. 'But he can pass on info to us and explain things to Inspector Acaster in more detail. We might have to tail her ourselves, but we can't do it dressed like this. She's already spotted us, and I suppose I stand out a *little* bit.'

Fi suppressed a snort. 'Let's assume she'll be in there for a while. Perhaps we have time to grab a change of clothes? She doesn't know the car.'

'Mmm,' said Jade. 'If the inspector gives her short shrift, she'll be out pretty soon. Besides, my clothes look like me and your clothes look like you. I've got a better idea. Didn't we pass a charity shop on the way here? Let's park opposite the car park exit, buy outfits and change, then wait. I've always wanted to wear a disguise.'

Ten minutes later, they squeezed into the Fiat. To

her disgust, Jade wore a pair of boot-cut corduroy trousers long enough to obscure her Doc Martens, a bottle-green ankle-length waxed raincoat and a matching waxed hat to hide her hair. Fi, equally disgusted, had swapped her comfortable trainers for a pair of black tasselled pixie boots and her well-fitting jacket for an oversized black hooded puffer that reached her knees.

'I look like a bin bag,' muttered Fi.

'I could hire myself out as a scarecrow,' complained Jade. 'Hang on, incoming call from Hugo. Yes… OK. Stay there. We'll follow at a discreet— Of course we'll be careful. Bye.' She turned to Fi. 'She's just leaving. There she is…'

Madeline, in her BMW, left the car park without noticing them and headed out of town. Fi started to worry. The courtesy car didn't have much fuel in the tank. If Madeline went any distance, they'd lose her. But after two minutes the BMW entered the supermarket car park. Fi and Jade parked at a distance and followed Madeline into the shop.

Fi hovered near the tills while Jade ambled about with a basket, picking things up and putting them down. Madeline, however, merely bought dog food and biscuits, then left. Watched closely by a security guard, Fi and Jade followed as slowly as they dared.

'I'm prepared to gamble that if she's getting dog stuff, she's going home,' said Fi, making less effort to keep the BMW in sight. She parked behind the Star and Fishes. 'Happy to continue on foot?'

'Yes,' said Jade. 'If she recognises me in this, I need to rethink my fashion sense.'

'Come on.' They headed down the lane.

Fi's heart thudded. What if her gamble was wrong and Madeline had left town? No, surely Inspector Acaster was right. Madeline had to keep up appearances. She'd wait for the funeral, at least, before she went away. But what could they do now?

They walked beyond the cottage as Madeline emerged from her car, then stopped at the post box, scrutinising the collection times. They heard a knock, followed by Madeline's voice. 'Hi. Sorry to bother you, but could I ask a favour?' She clearly wasn't addressing them.

Fi risked a peek and saw Madeline at an open door opposite the cottage, talking to another woman.

'It's a bit of an imposition given that he disturbs you, but could you dog-sit Basil this evening? Only… I'm finding things rather hard at the moment, and someone's asked me round for a quiet dinner. I really could do with it.' Her voice cracked. 'I just…'

'Yes, of course.'

'Oh, good,' said Madeline, a little more briskly. 'Here's the spare key and I've got your number. I'll let you know when I'm back.'

Before the neighbour could say anything else,

Madeline trotted across the road, collected the dog food from her car and entered the cottage.

'She's doing a runner, isn't she?' said Jade. 'I should know. I'm an expert.'

Fi tapped out a message on her phone. 'I've sent both car registrations to Inspector Acaster, and told her what we've heard.' Thirty seconds later, a reply flashed up. 'She's sending someone down. She says keep out of sight but keep an eye on things.'

'Shame I've forgotten the spell for invisibility,' muttered Jade. 'Next time, can we follow someone who lives somewhere busy?'

'Shh. Try and blend with the post box.'

'I'm green. It's red,' said Jade. 'If she's packing, she'll be upstairs. You keep watch and I'll rummage in her bins.' She pointed to the little shelter where they lived, on the opposite side from the Bains' parking space. 'There might be something worth finding, and I doubt she can see them from the house.'

'With your bare hands?' Fi made a face.

'Got gloves,' said Jade. She pushed up her sleeves and sidled towards the bins. Fi, wishing she had Stan as cover, wandered up and down the street, hoping she wouldn't bump into the neighbour who'd wanted the book on CCTV and have to have a complicated conversation at the wrong moment.

Less than five minutes passed before Madeline left the house with a wheeled suitcase and climbed into the Ferrari. She pulled away, giving a tiny wave, which Fi hoped was to Basil rather than her and Jade, drove along the lane and turned right.

Fi rang the inspector. 'She's left in the Ferrari with a suitcase and no dog, heading up London Road.'

'Right,' said Inspector Acaster. 'I'll send out an all-car alert and contact the next county too. Go home and I'll keep you posted. Er . . . thanks. Bye.'

Jade returned and held out three empty blister packs. 'Tell her I've found sleeping pills.'

'Too late,' said Fi. 'She's gone. Hang on, I've got plastic bags in my other jacket pocket. We can put them in that to prevent any more cross-contamination. The inspector says go home.'

'Humph,' said Jade. 'I'd suggest a pint at the pub if you weren't driving and we were wearing something sensible. Let's go to the boat, get changed and have a cuppa.'

In the Fiat, they shrugged off the loathed coats and Fi started for home.

Jade's phone rang. 'Hello? Er…' She turned to Fi. 'It's the inspector. How close are we to the train station? I've lost my bearings.'

'Five minutes, if that,' said Fi. 'Is Madeline there?'

'Yes. Picked up on the station CCTV.'

'Better change direction.' Cursing the learner driver and the bus in front of her, Fi negotiated a narrow street and did a three-point turn. At the station, she parked close to the Ferrari. The time for pretence was over, but all the same, she and Jade walked slowly towards the station. Madeline was standing by the cash machine as it churned out a wad of cash. She grabbed it and entered the building, wheeling her case, with Fi and Jade slinking in after her.

Fi looked at the departures board, dismissing the teenage girl waving a charity collection pot with an impatient hand. The next train to London, via Birmingham and Reading, was in four minutes, and if Fi remembered rightly, it only stopped at those three places. 'We mustn't let her buy a ticket!' she cried.

'How?' said Jade. 'She can get it from a machine. She might have already bought it on an app.'

'She'll want to pay cash so it's not as traceable.'

Madeline headed for the counter. On a whim, Fi grabbed the collection pot from the teenager, bounded up to Madeline and shoved it under her nose, shaking it frantically.

'What are you doing?' cried Madeline. 'Move!'

Jade snatched the teenager's leaflets and thrust one at her.

A disembodied, indifferent voice announced, 'The train now arriving at platform two is the London train—'

Madeline stared at the departures board, then the ticket office. Her eyes widened, and pushing Jade away, she made for the barriers. Fi stood in her way and Madeline's gaze hardened. 'These women are harassing me!' she yelled. 'Get the transport police! I have a train to catch.'

'Where is he?' asked Jade.

'Never you mind,' snapped Madeline.

'So you're admitting the body wasn't your husband?' said Fi.

Jade held up the plastic bag with the empty packets. 'Recognise these? Thought you'd know the council don't recycle blister packs.'

'What the— Get out of my way!' Madeline pushed her case at Jade and made a dash for the barrier. The ticket inspector on the other side gawped as she rushed towards him.

On the platform, the warning whistle blew.

'I'll buy my ticket through the app!' Madeline shouted. 'I must catch that train!'

Fi sprinted and grabbed her arm. 'I'm making a citizen's arrest!'

'Is that even a thing?' shouted Madeline, shaking Fi off. But just as Madeline was about to jump the barrier, Jade pulled her backwards and they landed in a tangle on the concourse.

Fi stood over them. 'If a citizen's arrest isn't a thing, it doesn't matter,' she said. 'Here's someone official. In fact, two.'

A transport police officer and a Hazeby constable

jostled for authority, then pulled Madeline to her feet. The police caution was barely audible over the final platform whistle and the train pulling out of the station.

Fi helped Jade up and turned to the teenage girl from the charity, who stood wide-eyed and open-mouthed. Fi handed her the collection tin as Jade gathered the scattered leaflets. 'Sorry about that: I'll give you some money. What are you collecting for?'

'St Jude's homeless shelter,' said the girl, dragging her gaze from Madeline being handcuffed and taking the crumpled leaflets from Jade. 'But it isn't just that. One of our regulars has been missing since just before Christmas. He left all his stuff, even his toothbrush, so he must have meant to come back. You haven't seen him, have you?'

She held up a leaflet and pointed at a picture of a man who was clearly in ill-health and down on his luck. In the photo his face was unshaven, undamaged and definitely alive. But Fi recognised him, though the only time she'd seen him, he'd been lying on a cold, ancient stone on midwinter's day.

CHAPTER 25

Jade put on her new earrings – silver moons, Hugo's Christmas present to her – and gave herself an approving glance in the mirror. For once she was wearing a dress, the colour of a ripe plum, with a deep V-neck and cut on the bias. *You'll do*, she told her reflection, and grabbed her bag.

On her way out, she paused and looked at the sofa. It seemed odd to have the flat to herself again. While it had been wonderful to see so much of Hugo, of course, being able to sprawl in her PJs and watch what she wanted was also very nice. *Enjoy it while you can*, she told herself. *Back to the daily grind soon enough.*

On impulse, she popped downstairs to the shop. It still stank of paint, but the walls glowed a deep, rich indigo and the new wood floor gleamed. She had chosen quality finishes, since she planned to stick around for many years to come. 'Much nicer,' said

Jade, and left before the fumes made her dizzy.

The street was full of revellers: everyone in party gear, talking, laughing and occasionally stumbling into the road. Jade suspected there was little chance of a quiet New Year drink anywhere. Hopefully Fi would agree and they could celebrate at *Coralie* with a couple of glasses of wine. However, as she started the descent towards the towpath, a figure crossed *Coralie*'s gangplank and resolved itself into Fi. 'Am I glad to see you,' she said, giving Jade a quick hug. 'They're so noisy.'

Jade grinned. 'How many friends have you let him have round?'

'Only four, but it feels like at least twenty. The sound bounces, and everywhere I go, I bump into one of them. Coming out of the bathroom, or looking in the fridge.'

'You're brave, leaving them alone.'

'I was very clear with Dylan about what will happen if anything is broken or anyone complains,' said Fi. 'I need time out for my own sanity.'

'Swan?' said Jade. 'It's not ticketed.'

'*Anywhere*.'

***

'Well, if it isn't the two heroes of the hour,' said Glenys.

Jade felt her cheeks begin to warm. 'It wasn't just us,' she said. 'The police were in charge. And my lad helped out, too.'

'I read the paper,' said Glenys. 'That Inspector Whatsits gave you a special mention.'

Jade couldn't help smiling. Later on the fateful day when Madeline Bain had been arrested at Hazeby station, Inspector Acaster had summoned her and Fi. 'If you're free, that is,' she said.

'I can be free,' said Jade. Indeed, she *was* free, sitting in Fi's galley kitchen with Hugo, while the three of them emptied a large pot of tea and tucked into doorstep sandwiches.

'I won't keep you long,' said Inspector Acaster, almost as soon as they had sat down. 'I wanted to thank you for your help. We didn't always see eye to eye—'

Jade snorted.

'However, both of you showed grit and determination, even when your lives and livelihoods were at stake. If there's anything I can do…'

'Thanks, Inspector, but I doubt it,' said Jade. 'Unless you happen to be best mates with a glazier and a decorator who are inexplicably free right now.'

Inspector Acaster tapped her pen on the desk. 'Not best mates, but maybe I can arrange something.' Two hours later, Jade had received three calls: two from tradespeople and one from a reporter at the local paper, asking her for a quote.

She jumped as Fi nudged her elbow. 'Jade, Glenys

is talking to you.'

'Hurry up and choose, love,' said Glenys. 'Free drinks don't come along every day.'

'Free drinks?' Jade gazed at the bar, flummoxed. 'What are you having, Fi?'

'White wine,' said Fi. 'A large one.'

'Me too, then.'

Glenys turned and took a bottle out of the fridge. 'We've got an offer on, so you can have the bottle.' She clunked it down on the bar. 'I'll get you an ice bucket.'

'Well,' said Fi, once they had wedged themselves in a corner and poured two glasses, 'this is nice.'

Jade surveyed the pub. Most of the tables were occupied, half with the usual clientele of steady pint drinkers, half with groups who hadn't managed to book anywhere and were drinking too fast. 'It's certainly a change,' she said, with a smile. 'So tell me, are you enjoying your peace and quiet?'

'What peace and quiet?' said Fi. 'I told you that reporter rang me too, didn't I?'

'You did.' Jade sipped her wine. The combination of ferocious central heating and an overcrowded pub made the atmosphere decidedly warm. She closed her eyes, savouring the drink, then opened them to find Fi gazing at her. 'Sorry, go on.'

'So he also asked if I fancied doing book reviews. A monthly round-up. I mean, I couldn't turn that down, could I? And the copy deadline's in a fortnight, so I need to get reading.'

'And you hate that, of course.'

'Very funny. But it's come just as I was reorganising the Book Barge. Loads of people come in wanting crime, mystery and thriller books, so I'm giving them more space. We won't be a specialist bookshop, but I'd be a fool to ignore demand.'

'That's brilliant! I'm so pleased for you!' Jade leaned over and put her arm round Fi. As she did so, she realised that she didn't feel even a twinge of jealousy. *Once, the thought of someone doing well would have eaten my heart out. And now... Once you don't have to scrabble around for every penny, it's much easier to believe that there's more to life than money.*

She blinked as Fi waved a hand in front of her face. 'Honestly, talk about away with the fairies.'

'Witches,' said Jade, automatically.

'Whatever. Are you enjoying being a lady of leisure? Or are you too busy missing your lodger?'

'I don't think Hugo will wait so long to visit in future.'

'Oh, so he likes Hazeby?'

'He does. Although next time he says he might stay in an Airbnb, since my sofa isn't as comfortable as a king-size bed. He stayed and supported me, though, bless him.' Jade opted not to mention that Hugo had asked her to invite Netta round to see her paint choices, made various incomprehensible remarks about colour theory, and given Netta his business card, which she had stuffed in her bag without looking at it. Frankly, Netta had been much more excited about selling the amethyst geode to someone in the crowd on the day of the fire. She chuckled at the memory. 'Want to see what I've been up to?' She unlocked her phone and showed Fi a series of photographs. A babbling brook, a bare tree in the snow, hills wreathed in mist, and a glorious sunrise, each in a simple wooden frame.

'Aww, those are nice,' said Fi. 'Did you take them yourself?'

Jade nodded. 'Before he left, Hugo took me on a photography outing. He even taught me how to use Photoshop. Well, he did most of it, to be honest.'

'And the frames? Rick?'

'Of course. He'll send people to me, and I'll send people to him. But all profit from these will go to St Jude's homeless shelter.'

'What a good idea,' said Fi, and covered Jade's hand with her own.

Rick had popped round earlier that day with a bottle bag. 'Belated Merry Christmas,' he said, holding it up.

'Wow, thank you.' Jade felt a pang of guilt that she hadn't bought him anything. Really, though, with a house guest and everything else that had happened, she thought she could be forgiven. 'Would you like to—'

'Can't stop,' said Rick. 'Me and the lads have got a gig in Spetisham tonight. Got to get over there for the sound check, then we're having our Christmas meal. I believe Christmas can be whenever you feel like it.'

'Me too.' On impulse, Jade stepped forward and hugged him. When she let go, he appeared stunned. 'Let's get together and have a drink sometime soon.'

'Um, yes. Yes, that would be nice.' He spent the next few seconds alternating between studying his feet and looking at Jade. 'I'd, um, better get on. Yes.' He took a couple of steps back, still gazing at her, then headed off.

'I thought I'd find you here,' said a familiar voice. Jade and Fi turned and saw Marcus Falconer, reprehensibly tanned and with sun-bleached hair, smiling.

'You're back!' cried Fi. 'Am I glad to see you!' She jumped up and threw her arms around him.

'She's glad to see everyone,' said Jade. 'But I must admit that I'm glad to see you too.'

'I'm just relieved you're both in one piece,' said Marcus. 'Honestly, a man heads off for a bit of rest and relaxation—'

'Leaving us to deal with Medusa,' said Jade.

Marcus grinned. 'She speaks highly of you.'

'There's a spare chair at that table,' said Fi. 'You grab that, Marcus, and I'll fetch another glass.'

Marcus raised his eyebrows, but did as he was told.

'How did you find us?' asked Jade.

'I popped along to *Coralie* to say hello and encountered noise levels which probably constitute a breach of the peace. I knocked on the door, ordered them to keep it down, and said that I wouldn't press charges if they told me where you were.'

'Excellent,' said Fi. 'So you've seen Inspector Acaster.'

'I have indeed. I'm not on duty till tomorrow, but I popped into the station for an informal handover. Nina spent about fifteen minutes telling me what a pair of undisciplined mavericks the pair of you were, then admitted she couldn't have done it without you. She even said she'd consider working with you again, which from her is high praise. She'll be back at Wyvernshire HQ tomorrow, putting the fear of God into everyone. Her chief's terrified of her.'

'Anything new to report?' asked Fi, filling his glass.

Marcus considered. 'I bought you a nice straw donkey.'

Fi rolled her eyes. 'About the case.'

Marcus settled back in his chair. 'They've got Bain. Turns out he was enjoying a bit of winter sun too in Malaga, marking time until Madeline could join him. He'll plead guilty – there's no point in him doing otherwise. Not with the file we've put together on this case and his money-laundering activities, thanks to a certain Hugo Fitch.' He winked at Jade. 'Useful young man, that.'

'He is,' said Jade. 'I believe Inspector Acaster has already recommended his services to other forces.'

Marcus raised his eyebrows. 'I imagine he charges a pretty penny. We were lucky to get him for free.' He swirled the wine in his glass. 'I have to say, though, I don't fancy Richard Bain's chances in jail. The gang he stole from don't take kindly to that sort of thing, and their networks stretch far and wide.'

Fi shivered. 'Let's talk about something else. What nice weather we're having for the time of year, or what we thought of the Christmas telly.'

'I know,' said Marcus, with a twinkle. 'New Year's resolutions.' He laughed at their groans. 'Mine is to take more breaks. I really enjoyed that holiday, despite your best efforts to scupper it.'

Fi sipped her wine, thinking hard. 'Mine is . . . to enjoy what I have. I'm very lucky and I don't always realise it.' She glanced at Jade. 'How about you? Turn over a million pounds? Solve another ten murders?'

Jade laughed, and drank some more wine. 'I will . . . worry less and enjoy my success,' she said firmly. 'I've predicted the failure of Crystal Dreams at least fifty times since it first opened, and it still hasn't happened. So I'll stop assuming that every little setback is a major crisis and trust in the universe.'

Marcus reached for the bottle of wine and pretended to sniff the top. 'Someone's got at your wine.'

'That's very rude,' said Jade, then giggled. 'Anyway, as you're holding the wine, fill 'em up and let's drink a toast. Here's to a new year and building on success. Cheers!'

Marcus topped up their wine and put his arm around Fi. 'Cheers,' they chorused, and clinked glasses. Jade took a hearty glug of wine, and thought that if the next year stayed pretty much like this, she would thoroughly enjoy it.

WHAT TO READ NEXT

If you've enjoyed reading Fi and Jade's third case together, watch out for the next book in the series: *Death on the Towpath.*

Fi and Jade are taking part in a fete at Spetisham Hall when a series of conversations suggest that Fi's dead husband isn't dead at all. Could it be true? And if it is, what does that mean for her and her son Dylan?

Before Fi has the chance to investigate, though, one of her informants is found dead at the river's edge.

If it's murder, who benefits apart from Fi? And is she in danger too?

Check out *Death on the Towpath* at http://mybook.to/Towpath.

If you've enjoyed reading a co-written book, Caster and Fleet Mysteries is a six-book series we wrote together, set in 1890s London. Meet Katherine and Connie, two young women who become friends in the course of solving a mystery together. Their unlikely partnership takes them to the music hall, masked balls, and beyond. Expect humour, a touch of romance, and above all, shenanigans!

The first book in the series is *The Case of the Black Tulips,* and you can read all about it here: http://mybook.to/Tulips.

If you love modern cozy mysteries set in rural England, *Pippa Parker Mysteries* is another six-book series set in and around the village of Much Gadding.

In the first book, *Murder at the Playgroup*, Pippa is a reluctant newcomer to the village. When she meets the locals, she's absolutely sure. There's just one problem; she's eight months pregnant.

The village is turned upside down when a pillar of the community is found dead at Gadding Goslings playgroup. No one could have murdered her except the people who were there. Everyone's a suspect, including Pippa…

With a baby due any minute, and hampered by her toddler son, can Pippa unmask the murderer?

Find *Murder at the Playgroup* here: http://mybook.to/playgroup.

Finally, if you love books and magic, welcome to

the *Magical Bookshop*! This six-book series combines mystery, magic, cats and of course books, and is set in modern London.

When Jemma James takes a job at Burns Books, the second-worst secondhand bookshop in London, she finds her ambition to turn it around thwarted at every step. Raphael, the owner, is more interested in his newspaper than sales. Folio the bookshop cat has it in for Jemma, and the shop itself appears to have a mind of its own. Or is it more than that?

The first in the series, *Every Trick in the Book*, is here: http://mybook.to/bookshop1

ACKNOWLEDGEMENTS

Our first thanks, as always, go to our wonderful beta readers – Carol Bissett, Ruth Cunliffe, Christine Downes, Stephen Lenhardt, Carmen Radtke and Julia Smith – and to our keen-eyed and indefatigable proofreader, John Croall. Thank you all for your assistance! Any errors that remain are our responsibility.

And many thanks to you, dear reader! We hope you've enjoyed the latest instalment in Fi and Jade's adventures. If you have, please consider leaving a short review or a rating on Amazon and/or Goodreads. Reviews and ratings are very important to authors, as they help books to find new readers.

COVER CREDITS

Image: Depositphotos.

Cover fonts:

Fairing by Design and Co.

Dancing Script OT by Impallari Type: https://www.fontsquirrel.com/fonts/dancing-script-ot. License: SIL Open Font License v1.10: http://scripts.sil.org/OFL.

ABOUT LIZ HEDGECOCK

Liz Hedgecock grew up in London, England, did an English degree, and then took forever to start writing. After several years working in the National Health Service, some short stories crept into the world. A few even won prizes. Then the stories started to grow longer…

Now Liz travels between the nineteenth and twenty-first centuries, murdering people. To be fair, she does usually clean up after herself.

Liz's reimaginings of Sherlock Holmes, her Pippa Parker cozy mystery series, the Caster & Fleet Victorian mystery series (with Paula Harmon), the Magical Bookshop series, and the Maisie Frobisher Mysteries are available in ebook and paperback.

Liz lives in Cheshire with her husband and two sons, and when she's not writing or child-wrangling you can usually find her reading, messing about on

Twitter, or cooing over stuff in museums and art galleries. That's her story, anyway, and she's sticking to it.

Website/blog: http://lizhedgecock.wordpress.com
Facebook: http://www.facebook.com/lizhedgecockwrites
Twitter: http://twitter.com/lizhedgecock
Goodreads: https://www.goodreads.com/lizhedgecock

ABOUT PAULA HARMON

Paula Harmon is a civil servant, living in Dorset, married with two adult children. Paula has several writing projects underway and wonders where the housework fairies are, because the house is a mess and she can't think why.

For book news, offers and even the occasional recipe, please sign up to my newsletter via my website.

https://paulaharmon.com
viewauthor.at/PHAuthorpage
https://www.facebook.com/pg/paulaharmonwrites
https://www.goodreads.com/paula_harmon
https://twitter.com/Paula_S_Harmon

BOOKS BY LIZ HEDGECOCK

To check out any of my books, please visit my Amazon author page at http://author.to/LizH. If you follow me there, you'll be notified whenever I release a new book.

The Magical Bookshop (6 novels)

An eccentric owner, a hostile cat, and a bookshop with a mind of its own. Can Jemma turn around the second-worst secondhand bookshop in London? And can she learn its secrets?

Pippa Parker Mysteries (6 novels)

Meet Pippa Parker: mum, amateur sleuth, and resident of a quaint English village called Much Gadding. And then the murders began…

Booker & Fitch Mysteries (3 novels, with Paula Harmon)

Jade Fitch hopes for a fresh start when she opens a new-age shop in a picturesque market town. Meanwhile, Fi Booker runs a floating bookshop as well as dealing with her teenage son. And as soon as they meet, it's murder…

Caster & Fleet Mysteries (6 novels, with Paula Harmon)

There's a new detective duo in Victorian London . . . and they're women! Meet Katherine and Connie, two young women who become partners in crime. Solving it, that is!

Mrs Hudson & Sherlock Holmes (3 novels)

Mrs Hudson is Sherlock Holmes's elderly landlady. Or is she? Find out her real story here.

Maisie Frobisher Mysteries (4 novels)

When Maisie Frobisher, a bored young Victorian socialite, goes travelling in search of adventure, she finds more than she could ever have dreamt of. Mystery, intrigue and a touch of romance.

Sherlock & Jack (3 novellas)

Jack has been ducking and diving all her life. But when she meets the great detective Sherlock Holmes they form an unlikely partnership. And Jack discovers that she is more important than she ever realised…

Halloween Sherlock (3 novelettes)

Short dark tales of Sherlock Holmes and Dr Watson, perfect for a grim winter's night.

For children

A Christmas Carrot (with Zoe Harmon)

Perkins the Halloween Cat (with Lucy Shaw)

Rich Girl, Poor Girl (for 9-12 year olds)

BOOKS BY PAULA HARMON

THE MURDER BRITANNICA SERIES

Murder Mysteries set in 2nd Century Britain

mybook.to/MurderBritanniaSeries

THE MARGARET DEMERAY SERIES

Historical Mysteries set in the lead-up to World War 1

mybook.to/MargaretDemeraySeries

OTHER BOOKS BY PAULA HARMON

https://paulaharmon.com/books-by-paula-harmon/

SHORT STORIES BY PAULA HARMON & VAL PORTELLI

viewbook.at/PHWeirdandpeculiartales

AUDIOBOOKS BY PAULA HARMON

https://paulaharmon.com/audiobooks/

WHITE
RHINO
BOOKS

Printed in Great Britain
by Amazon

26454446R10138